LADY RAGS

EDIE JOHNSON

PAGE PUBLISHING, INC.
Conneaut Lake, PA

First originally published by Page Publishing 2020

ISBN 978-1-64334-912-1 (pbk)
ISBN 978-1-64334-911-4 (digital)

Printed in the United States of America

1

Gil pushed aside strings of sticky cobwebs as he explored the abandoned hotel's decayed dining room. The notion of a scurrying spider falling down inside his coat collar added nothing to Gil's grim appreciation of the moldy waterfront building.

"We must be crazy, Gil," Pam Hayworth said from close behind her husband. "When I think of all I could be doing at home on a rainy Saturday morning…" She shivered. "Let's get out of here."

"I know the old woman lives in here, Pam. I followed her here in the car yesterday." He tested each rotting floor board cautiously with his foot, avoiding those that had already cracked beneath the weight of a previous explorer.

The Grand Hotel's condition saddened Gil. With his heightened imagination, as Pam frequently called it, he could almost see the place as it had been in its heyday—when the shipping trade had brought prestigious visitors to Grayport on business. Sailing vessels and great cargo ships had sailed into the harbor and up to the mouth of the Chehalis River, where tugboats had assisted them to the docks and to their journey's end. From passenger ships, men, women, and children had disembarked and made their way to the Grand Hotel. Cargo ships had stopped long enough to unload goods for the adventurous who had begun to settle the coastal communities or to load shipments of lumber from the many sawmills that had sprung up along the coast. Large numbers of trees were cut from the vast forests of the Pacific Northwest then were loaded and shipped back to the east coast or to ports around the world.

Guests at the hotel would have dined in the enormous room that Gil and Pam now explored. Gil wished that the walls were able to tell what they had seen and heard—the conversations at tables covered with gleaming white linen tablecloths and elegantly arrayed with crystal and silver, the rustle of long silk dresses as the ladies moved across the polished hardwood floor. What echoes of laughter did the old hotel walls conceal? What sobs from a broken heart did it hide in the silent walls? What tragic secrets still lurked in the shadows of the now deserted rooms?

"Too bad this place was left to rot," Pam said, breaking into Gil's thoughts. "It would have made a wonderful museum."

Gil agreed, but the Grand Hotel was a sore subject with Grayport's city fathers. The disagreements about the building's future still divided city council members, whether new to the position or the old timers. The hotel's last owner had deeded the hotel, and the chunk of harbor property it sat upon, to the City of Grayport after his own restoration funds had failed to materialize, and the city had refused him permission to demolish it. Now the city had no restoration or demolition funds either. Consequently, the building's condition worsened with each passing year.

"Come on. Let's look upstairs." Gil motioned for Pam to follow him.

"Gil, I'm not going up those steps. They're ready to fall in."

He had already started to climb the broad, winding staircase, testing each step for strength. "No, they aren't, Pam. If you look closely, you'll see there are no cobwebs. Someone uses these stairs quite regularly."

Pam was not thrilled with that idea either. There could be someone upstairs who would not appreciate their company, someone with a gun or knife. That thought, along with the cold rain blowing in the gaping holes where windows once were and the smell of decay, only added to Pam's discomfort. She shivered again, wishing now that she hadn't agreed to come along with Gil on this misadventure.

She had been hearing about Grayport's bag lady for over a month now from her colleagues at the elementary school where she worked in the office. Even a few students had remarked that they had seen her shuffling into an alley as they were on the way to or from school. Pam's curiosity had not been aroused in the slightest. She guessed that the old woman must live in one of the shabby apartment houses behind the Pick'N Pack supermarket and that she was perfectly able to take care of herself.

Gil thought differently. Customers in his pharmacy had been talking about her, wondering why she had suddenly appeared in Grayport. He had not seen the woman himself until two days earlier when she'd shuffled across the street in front of his car when he stopped at a downtown stoplight.

The day had been gray and misty, and he'd thought he was seeing an apparition. Her tall, thin frame was garbed in a Navy foul weather jacket over a long, billowy black skirt made from some shiny fabric that Gil didn't recognize. She pushed a rickety baby stroller that was overburdened with more wares than the wobbly wheels could tolerate. He had stared as she passed in front of his car and kept staring as she disappeared down the sidewalk into the alley. For two days, he had not been able to get the pathetic, yet somehow comical, sight out of his head. And even though her head had been covered by a black southwester, and he didn't get a good look at her face, the image of Ichabod Crane kept coming to mind.

Later that morning, the subject of the bag lady had come up again among his customers. No one could understand why she would just show up in a place like Grayport. The average rainfall in a normal year exceeded seventy inches, and even the locals complained about the lack of sunshine during the fall and winter months. Some summers even boasted more rainfall than sunshine which made the natives grumpy.

"If I see a rat, I'm leaving!" Pam hissed, bringing Gil back to the present.

He reached around and took her hand in his as they continued to the top of the staircase. He knew the possibility of seeing various types of rodents was great, but he didn't tell Pam that. She had not been enchanted about searching for the bag lady with him, and he thought it a miracle when she'd finally relented. Once upon a time, Pam would have gone anywhere with him just so they could be together, but to Gil's consternation, that had changed. The children were older now, and Pam had interests of her own. He missed her enthusiasm for things he enjoyed. Nevertheless, they were close to a discovery now, in this upper hallway, and he wasn't going to quit now, rats or no rats.

They crept quietly along the wide corridor, peering into empty rooms as they went. Faded flowered wallpaper was peeling off the walls in every room, and green mold clung to everything. There was no glass in any of the windows, and shredded damask draperies blew in and out with the wind and the rain, their elegance long forgotten.

"There's no one up here, Gil." Pam tugged at his coat sleeve, hoping to stop him from going one step farther. "Can we just go now?"

"I just want to go to the end of the hall while we're here. I know she came into this building."

After leaving work that night, on the day he'd first spotted the old lady, he had driven around town, hoping to spot her on the street. Just as he was ready to give up, and he was hopelessly late for dinner, he had seen her on River Street headed for the Grand Hotel. He had turned off his headlights and inched the car slowly along the curb, watching as she pushed her battered stroller to the hotel's unhinged front door and disappeared inside the dark building.

"Gil, there's still another floor above us. Some of those old transients could be holed up in this building.

"I know, but I don't think she'd haul that cart of hers up too many flights of stairs, and I didn't see it down below."

"Maybe she just came in to get out of the drizzly weather that night. It's too cold and damp in here for her to stay here long."

"Maybe so, but I still want to look."

"Well, just remember, if you fall through the floor and break a leg, I'm not staying home to take care of you."

Gil believed her, but he had no intention of breaking anything. "As soon as we've looked into these last few rooms, we'll go." He stopped suddenly and signaled for her to be quiet. "Someone's moving around in that room," he whispered, pointing toward the last room in the hall, the only room that still boasted a door with hinges intact.

"What are we going to do?" she whispered, clutching at his sleeve.

"We're going to find out who's in there."

They stood frozen in the hallway, waiting for someone or something to emerge from the room. When no one appeared and the shuffling noises had stopped, Gil moved slowly toward the door and knocked gently. There were no answering sounds. He squatted down and peeked through the holes where the doorknob and keyhole cover had once been. There was no one there. He pushed the door, and it creaked open on rusty hinges. Gil moved slowly into the room, Pam close on his heels.

"We have no business being here, Gil. You're going to get us killed." She could just see the headlines in the local paper: Pharmacist and Wife Murdered in Grand Hotel!

"There's no one here, Pam. Relax!"

Gil ignored her pleas and began, cautiously, investigating the room. The stroller piled with miscellaneous goods was just inside the door. Farther in, there was a sink, but no running water; there were electrical outlets, but no power. Cooking facilities consisted of a two-burner propane stove with one workable burner, a dented aluminum pan which was still on the stove with dried food caked on the bottom, and a battered coffeepot half full of the cold black brew. An assortment of chipped or cracked dishes was on a shelf over the sink, and mismatched silverware, unwashed, was in the sink. A round three-legged table, with one short leg, had been placed in the center of the room. It was covered with a faded, worn tablecloth that Gil decided had been pink at one time. Set in the center of the table was an empty Jack Daniel's bottle with one white plastic daisy stuck in it. Beside the table was one old wooden chair. Another chair with all of its legs sawed off by several inches sat nearby. A cot with an old feather tick-type mattress, several threadbare quilts, and two army blankets covering it, was shoved against the wall farthest from the canvas-covered window.

Gil went to the window and pulled back the heavy canvas that had been partially nailed over it to keep out the wind and the rain. Outside the window, an iron balcony clung precariously to the hotel's clapboard exterior, most of its rusty nails coming loose and falling to the ground. An iron ladder led down from the balcony to the rocky shore below. Seagulls squawked loudly as they circled overhead. Gil decided that someone had just made a hasty departure from the room by way of the shaky ladder, sending the gulls into their frenzied flight.

"I don't see her anywhere," Gil told Pam.

"What if it wasn't her?"

"I'd be willing to bet that it is her. Check out the army boots under the cot. She was wearing boots like those, and those have been worn recently."

He dropped the canvas back over the window and went to examine the room's second window. It also looked out over the river and was covered with canvas. Unlike the first though, the second window still had dangerous shards of glass clinging to its frame.

"Quite a setup," he remarked, dropping the second canvas back into place. "A little too cold and damp for my taste, but still she has almost everything she needs."

Pam sat down on the one and only chair at the table and tenderly touched the faded daisy. "How lonely she must be," she said, sadly, "and why here, Gil? Why not at the Mission where it's warm and food is provided?"

"I don't know, Pam. I've wondered the same thing myself. I'd also like to know where she came from and how she ended up in Grayport just recently."

He wandered around the small room, looking into the adjoining doorless rooms, finding nothing. These rooms seemed too small to have been one of the hotel's finer suites. One of the adjoining rooms had once been a bathroom, but all the plumbing and fixtures had long since been removed. Gil wondered what the old woman did without bathroom facilities. He squelched the thought that she might be polluting the river. Besides, that would be too cold and too inconvenient.

"Can we get out of here now, Gil? You wouldn't like someone poking around your home, snooping through your stuff."

"That would be a little different, Pam."

"Why? Trespassing is trespassing."

He remembered the bright red "No Trespassing" signs that were posted all over the building's exterior walls.

"She trespassed here first." He laughed.

"This isn't funny, Gil. We shouldn't be here, and I'm leaving." She got up and headed for the door. Gil followed, knowing that any more investigating would have to be done on his own. Pam wasn't interested.

*****

Mollie waited in her hiding place at the bottom of the hotel's rickety fire escape until she was sure that the intruders in her room were long gone. The fear that the man might decide to climb down the ladder, searching for her, had nearly stopped her heart. She looked at her feet and moaned. Her boots were still in the room, and the three pair of woolen socks on her feet were soaking wet. Dry socks didn't come easy, but Mollie was sure she still had a few pair in the old cardboard box of clothes she had stashed under the sink. If there was one thing she hated, it was wet feet.

Thank goodness she'd had time to put on her raincoat before the intruders got into her room. Otherwise, the rest of her would be soaked too. She hoisted herself back up the shaky ladder, wrapping her numb toes, in soggy socks, around each rung as she went and fighting the long, wet skirt that wrapped itself around her legs. Her rough, nearly tumbling descent earlier had left her feeling sore and bruised. All she wanted now was to get back into her room without any more trouble.

When she reached the balcony, she was able, with much huffing and puffing, to get through the window and stand upright in her room again. Nothing was missing that she could see, but knowing someone had snooped through her stuff was unsettling. Why had she had visitors all of a sudden? She puzzled over it while she dug into the cardboard box for dry socks. Was someone going to force her to move on just when she was getting acquainted with Grayport? It wasn't fair. She knew which restaurants and grocery stores tossed out the good food, and she knew just when to be there to get the best pickings. She shook her head. It would be a shame to have to leave that all behind and start over again somewhere else—somewhere where she'd have to fight with other street people for every scrap.

It wasn't so bad here. Not like Portland or down in California. Sure, the damp weather kept her bones aching, but she hoped it was a temporary condition. She had heard that western Washington State had mild temperatures, and when the rain passed, it might warm up. She didn't think that she had the strength to move on again now. *Maybe they were just exploring,* she thought to herself. *It probably wasn't the welfare people or anyone trying to socialize me.* It wasn't the police, she was sure of that. They knew she lived in the hotel, and they usually kept an eye out for her even though they couldn't tell anyone that. It was just something she knew.

She threw her dripping black slicker over the chair and patted her wet hair and face with the remains of an old towel. The cold had already crept into her bones. She unfastened the black skirt and let it fall to the floor, exposing the floral-patterned long johns underneath. After draping the skirt carefully over the kitchen chair to dry, she lay down on the cot and tugged the assortment of quilts and blankets up under her chin. Soon the warmth from her own body encircled her, and she slept in spite of her fear that the visitor might return.

2

With some disappointment, Gil accepted Pam's disinterest in Lady Rags. After all, she was busy trying to meet the needs of three teenage children, busy keeping their two-story Colonial-style home in some semblance of order, and busy with her job in the principal's office at McCausland Elementary School.

He had, however, expected to generate interest in the old woman from his longtime friend, Harv Olafson, the editor of the *Daily Register*, Grayport's only newspaper. But even Harv was less than understanding. When Harv came into the drugstore the day after Halloween, Gil saw him coming and knew that he was coming to refill his gout medicine. While Gil counted out pills, he asked Harv, "Any troubles last night with vandals or doctored candy?"

"Actually, it was pretty quiet this year. The schools had parties, so that helped some."

"I was just thinking about that old bag lady that wanders around. I hope no one decided she was a good target to terrorize."

"You dumb Irishman," Harv exclaimed. "What's gotten into you? Ellie told me you'd been interested in that old lady lately."

Gil was used to being called an Irishman, but it stemmed more from his red hair and ruddy complexion than from his ancestry. Fortunately, the flaming red hair and freckles of his youth had mellowed into more of a russet color with age, and he was more satisfied with the tall, blue-eyed man that looked back at him each morning as he shaved. At least he had a thick crop of hair which was more than Harv's gleaming bald head could boast. And Harv was the only person in the world who could call Gil "dumb."

"How did Ellie know?" Gil knew even before he asked that Harv's wife had talked to Pam. The two women were good friends and talked on the phone often.

"Ellie knows all, sees all, tells all, don't you know? Anyhow, I've never known you to show any particular interest in any other street people in this town, except the ones you have for customers."

"There's something different about this old woman, Harv. It's hard to explain." He told Harv about how he and Pam had searched the Grand Hotel.

"Buddy, you really are crazy! I've seen the old woman a couple of times myself, but she didn't impress me much, certainly not enough to make me follow her around town." He thought for a minute. "You know, I did wonder if she might really be a man, like undercover or something."

"So she did whet your imagination?" Gil laughed again. "I knew you'd be looking for a good story there somewhere."

"I just thought with all the drug problems cropping up, who'd pay attention to an old crone like that? 'Course who knew you'd take a liking to her? You're just liable to blow his cover."

"I don't think she's a man in disguise. Would a man put an old plastic flower in a vase on the table?"

"It would be a nice touch. Throw anyone off who might be looking for a drug enforcer."

"I still don't think so." Gil shook his head as he handed Harv his prescription. "Call it instincts."

"Maybe she's a retired hooker. I've often wondered where they go when they get too old."

"Harv, I don't think they get too old. Look at Maizie." Maizie was a customer who was in her nineties and always had a pretty young lady with her when she came into the store. It was no secret that she was still operating as a madam, but nothing was being done to put her out of business. "No, I don't think the bag lady's a hooker."

"What did Pam think of your little adventure?"

"Not much. She would agree with you totally, that I am crazy."

"See, I knew Pam had some brains, even if she did choose you for a husband."

"I'll tell her at dinner that you sent your 'regards.'" Gil scoffed.

Harv laughed and slapped his leg. "You do that!" He turned to leave. "We should be having a good clam tide one of these days. Maybe we can all go clam digging together again."

That would be an outing that Gil knew Pam and the kids would enjoy. When the Hayworths and the Olafsons got together, everyone had fun.

"Good idea!" he told his friend as Harv turned and headed for the front of the store. "I'll let you know when the next good clam tide is," he hollered back over his shoulder.

Both Gil and Harv had been born and raised in Grayport, and both had married college sweethearts then returned to Grayport to start their careers. They were the unusual ones. Most of their school friends had been glad to leave Grayport's gloomy weather behind and return only to visit.

Gil liked the moderate Western Washington climate, even with the rain, and a day at the nearby beaches, breathing the salt air of the Pacific Ocean, was an exhilarating and enjoyable day for him.

It was dark and cold by the time Gil closed the drugstore that evening. Pam had called to ask him to stop on his way home for milk, something he often did, but this time he did more willingly, trying to please Pam. He chose the Pick'N Pack supermarket which wasn't exactly on his way but was the store he preferred to the other super-markets in town. It was only a few blocks from the drugstore and the only large market still located in the downtown shopping core.

On his way out of the supermarket's Front Street entrance, a gallon of milk in each hand, he nearly tripped over the rickety baby stroller that Lady Rags shoved in front of him. Surprised, Gil stared into her weathered face, and the image of Ichabod Crane evaporated. This woman had been beautiful at one time, her face showing only signs of years without beauty creams. She stared back at him with sad, watery blue eyes—eyes that were startled now because he was so close. The hooked nose he'd visualized was actually perfectly shaped, only red and chapped like her cheeks. Tendrils of gray hair escaped from under the knitted wool cap that covered her head. She frantically shoved the cart out of his way, and, grunting unintelligibly, she disappeared around a dark corner of the supermarket.

Gil was shaken by the encounter. Why had it affected him so badly? Maybe Harv was right. Maybe he was crazy. After all, she was on old bag lady, minding her own business and, more than likely, wanted to be left alone.

He drove around the block twice and down River Street past the Grand Hotel, but he couldn't find her again. He circled the block two more times, but Lady Rags was nowhere to be seen.

*****

In the shadows behind the Pick'N Pack where Mollie hid, she watched as the white car drove slowly by as though the driver searched for something or someone. She was sure it was the same car that had been parked at the old Grand the day those people went into her room. What did they want with her?

Must she now be on guard all the time? She had felt safe in Grayport in the short time since she'd arrived. No one paid any attention to her. No one had tried to beat her up. The police didn't hassle her.

She waited, afraid to start walking toward the hotel. There were no trees, no buildings, only a block-long vacant lot between her and the old Grand. There would be no place to hide. The white car passed by again. A cold wind off the river blew through her hiding place and made Mollie shiver. She was used to being cold and wet. At least the rain had stopped for two whole days. Now she was just cold. The rain was the really unbearable thing about life in Grayport. Mollie had never seen so much rain or lived where it rained so much. At least she didn't remember if she had. *No wonder the people on the streets always seemed to be packin' umbrellas.*

When she was sure that the car had finished circling the block, she pushed her cart out of the shadows and headed toward the hotel, hurrying in case the car came back. When she was safely inside the hotel, she left her cart at the bottom of the dark stairs, pulled her flashlight out of her pocket, and slowly climbed up to the second floor. She was exhausted. *Lordy, Lordy, what a night!*

*****

Gil was anxious to tell Pam all about his encounter, but the family was already sitting down at the kitchen table when he came in the back door.

"Am I late?" he asked, seeing Pam glance at the kitchen clock.

"A little, and the kids need to eat. Traci is babysitting at the Palmer's, and Tim has a game. Boyd has to get going pretty soon too."

"I know," Gil put in. "He's driving Jason, Mark, Greg, and Brian to Seattle, in *your* van so they can all get a look at the girls on the university's campus." Gil laughed, remembering his eldest son's upcoming weekend adventure. "I'm not sure, Pam, if I'd want my car used in such an escapade."

Boyd blushed, a trait he hated and had never lived down with his friends.

"Dad, that's not why we're going." Then he grinned. "At least that's not the *only* reason we're going."

Boyd, tall and fair like his mother, was finishing his second year at Grayport's community college and wanted to attend the university next year. He and his friends had been invited to visit the campus to look things over. Since he was an excellent student and he had never given his parents any problems, Gil had no doubt that Boyd had a promising future in whatever he chose to do and that he would be accepted at the university. There was even a good chance he'd receive a basketball scholarship. It would be hard to see him leave home when the time came, but Gil had great confidence in the young man.

Gil sat down at his place at the end of the kitchen table, opposite Pam, and dished chicken casserole onto his plate. "Guess who I saw at the supermarket," Gil said, trying not to make it sound like a big deal.

"I'm too tired for guessing games, Gil," Pam told him. "Why don't you just tell us?"

"I saw that old bag lady. She nearly run me down with her cart, and you know…"

"Gil, are you still on that kick?" Pam snapped. "I had hoped you'd forgotten about her."

"I'm not on any 'kick,' Pam. I'm just interested. Is that so bad?"

"Maybe not. I'm sorry," she apologized. "It's just that it's Friday night and I still have Tim's game to get through before I can sit down and relax."

Tim, their high school junior, spoke up. "If Mom don't like my games, Dad," he said, mockingly. "Maybe you can take your ugly old girlfriend."

The remark infuriated Gil. Tim's attitude of late had been increasingly unbearable. Unlike his older brother, Tim had given them more anxious moments in the last few months than they cared to have in a lifetime. "Your mother likes your games. Don't be so insolent," Gil said to his son.

"No, she doesn't," he barked. "Just ask her."

"All I said was it's hard for a mother to watch her son getting his brains beat out at those football games," Pam explained.

"What has gotten into you, Pam? I've always thought you enjoyed both Tim and Boyd's games. Besides, Tim is tough. He wouldn't be a center on the team if he wasn't." Unlike Boyd, Tim had his father's ruddy complexion and red hair and a shorter, more muscular frame which suited him for football.

Suddenly, Pam looked like she might cry, so Gil dropped the subject, vowing to pursue it later. There was more to Pam's distress than she was saying.

"It was really something though, seeing the bag lady up close like that," Gil continued as he ate. "Harv thinks she's really a man, maybe an undercover cop." He looked around the table. From the sour expressions on all their faces, talking about the bag lady was obviously still not a good idea.

"Would someone please tell me what's going on?"

"How can we, Dad?" Tim smirked. "All you care about is your smelly girlfriend."

"That's not true, Tim, and you know it. Besides, you're always talking about that Nickerson kid, who, in my estimation, is nothing but a thug."

"He's not a thug. He just knows how to have a good time. But if it will make you feel better, I'm interested in a girl. I'm going to ask Cathy Southern to the homecoming dance. I think she likes me."

Fourteen-year-old Traci nearly choked on a mouthful of casserole. "She doesn't even know you're alive, creep. And she never will as long as you hang out with Bailey Nickerson. He's an even bigger creep than you are."

Gil spoke sharply to both of them. "Stop it! Let's just finish this meal in silence, okay?"

"That's hard to do with old metal mouth sitting next to me," Tim scoffed. Traci had just recently acquired a mouthful of braces. The girl's eyes filled with tears, and she abruptly left the table.

Gil, usually a nonviolent man, wanted to thrash his young son. "Tim, leave this table immediately and apologize to your sister before you take one step out of this house."

Tim shoved his chair back and stomped doggedly out of the kitchen. A few minutes later, the front door slammed, and Tim's car roared out of the driveway and screeched down the hill toward town.

No one said anything. Gil knew he'd lost another round with his second son. He'd lost quite a few since the boy had started running with Bailey Nickerson. It hurt both Gil and Pam to have Tim on this seemingly destructive course but neither knew how to cope with the problem. It was one of those things that happened in other people's families, but not in your own.

Boyd stood up and patted his stomach. "Good dinner, Mom. Now I'd better get my things together and go pick up the guys."

"Would you check on Traci while you're upstairs?" Pam asked Boyd. "Tell her I'll be up in a minute."

"Sure, Mom, but I'm sure she's all right. We both know we have a turkey for a brother."

After Boyd had gone upstairs, Pam put her face in her hands and began to cry. Gil moved closer and put his arm around her. "It'll be all right. Tim will wise up pretty soon and realize what kind of a kid Bailey Nickerson really is."

"What kind of a kid *is* Bailey Nickerson, Gil? We think he's a thug. Tim thinks he's a great friend. We've heard stories about how wild he is. Tim says the stories aren't true."

"I think we have to look at Tim's attitude since he's been running with Nickerson and his friends. He isn't learning that stuff at home."

"Do you think they're into drugs?"

"I think Tim is smarter than that. At least I hope so."

"But we thought he was a nice, regular kid until the beginning of this school year when Bailey Nickerson appeared in town again. He has proven us wrong there."

"You just want him to be like Boyd, and that is never going to happen. Tim is a different kid altogether. Remember when they were in Little League? Boyd was every coach's favorite kid. Tim was a prankster who made the other kids laugh but annoyed the coaches. Maybe even now, he's just trying to stay out of Boyd's shadow and do his own thing. For some outlandish reason, the Nickerson kid must give Tim the opportunity to do that."

Pam thought about it. "I hope you're right. Remember when a broken shoestring could ruin Tim's whole day while nothing much ruffled Boyd's feathers. Boyd has had many friends over the years while Tim has only had Dave Doyle. I wonder what happened between Tim and Dave."

"I think Bailey Nickerson happened between them. Dave was not included when Nickerson started up a friendship with Tim."

"How sad. I'd like to know just why the Nickerson boy wanted to befriend Tim. According to Traci, he had guys clamoring to ride in that souped-up van of his. She thought they were all nuts. I think she was surprised when Tim became one of those guys."

"Pam, we have raised Tim the same as the others. He's a good kid with good moral values. I hope, no, I pray that good sense will win out before he gets into anything that will cost him those values."

"You'd better be right, Gil. I can't take much more of the abuse and sullenness that kid brings into this house."

"So how about a movie tonight?"

"Gil, you know we've got a football game to go to."

"I thought you didn't like football games."

"I'm a mother. I can squawk about them if I want to, but he'd be disappointed if we didn't show up."

"Okay, maybe we'll see a movie tomorrow night." Gil decided that perhaps Tim wasn't the only contrary person in the household.

"That would be nice. Just as long as it isn't *My Fair Lady*."

Gil got the message. No one seemed to understand his motives for Lady Rags, but how could they? Gil didn't understand them either.

3

As the gray clouds and steady drizzle intensified into black clouds and wind-driven rain, the mood around Grayport by mid-November was anything but cheerful. Even Gil began to feel the effects of the dreary, sunless days. He complained right along with his customers about the absence of blue skies and sunshine. His concern wasn't just for himself though. He was concerned about the old woman who made her way around Grayport's streets scavenging for food. How was she doing? He'd stopped looking for her, mainly to keep peace in the family and because he had other more pressing problems to deal with.

Tim had been suspended from school for a week because school officials found a bag of marijuana in his locker. Tim denied that it belonged to him, swearing that he didn't use the stuff and never would. Gil and Pam wanted to believe him in spite of the strength of the evidence, but they also didn't want to be naive parents who thought their child would never do anything wrong. They were intelligent enough to know that two or more kids together sometimes feel invincible and think nothing in the world can touch them. Tim was finding out differently.

His week off from school was touching him in ways that didn't allow him any television, telephoning his friends, or driving his car. Gil made up a list of jobs he wanted done by the end of the week, and so far Tim had made progress. He'd raked up dead and rotting leaves, replaced two boards in the picket fence that separated the backyard from the alley, and he'd repaired a broken front step. He'd also had coffee brewing and the table set every night when Pam came home at four o'clock from her job at the school. The fact that Tim didn't complain about the work or that he was missing football practice every day and would miss the game on Friday night encouraged Gil. Perhaps there was an inkling of respect buried somewhere in their son's tough exterior.

On the following rainy Monday morning, the Hayworth family returned to normal. Tim left for school in his car, Pam dropped Traci off at the junior high, and Gil gave Boyd a lift downtown to the popular Ho Hum Café so he could catch a ride out to the college with his friend, Jason. Boyd was temporarily between cars. He'd sold his '57 Chevy to a high school kid and was looking for something better to drive to the university next year. He had his eye on a 1992 Dodge Dart, but Gil didn't think Boyd's funds would go that far. Even though he'd been working at a busy gas station after school, weekends, and summers since his junior year of high school, Gil thought that Boyd probably didn't put enough in the bank to afford a car. After all, there were other things to spend it on, like girls.

Gil could barely see through the sheet of rain that pounded his windshield. There was no place to park in front of the Ho Hum, so he pulled in close to let Boyd out. As he was pulling back into traffic, he saw a familiar figure emerge from the alley next to the café. He strained forward in his seat, trying to see past the clacking windshield wipers and the steady downpour. The woman, clad in the black raincoat with a seaman's southwester pulled down over her head, shuffled slowly, in oversize green boots, across the busy street, heedless of the cars that had to slow up to avoid hitting her. Gil held his breath until she was safely on the other side of the street, and he watched as she disappeared into the alley. Why did he feel so responsible for her? It wasn't a latent mother-son problem that made the old woman important to him. In fact, if his mother knew about the bag lady, she'd question his sanity and side with Pam in the matter. Those two always stuck together in everything.

After his father's death five years ago, his mother had grieved for eight months, sometimes alone and sometimes very loudly with Gil and Pam. Then one day she stopped grieving, packed up, and went on a cruise with two of her widowed friends, and she's been cruising ever since. She was somewhere in Europe at that moment, touring with five of her friends, having the time of her life. Occasionally, she'd send them a card or call, but usually they heard nothing.

As Gil pulled into the parking lot adjacent to the drugstore, he spotted the wooden sign that swung in the wind and rain in front of Ostergood's Flower Shop, two doors down. He knew the shop wasn't open yet, but Mr. Ostergood was always there. He lived upstairs over the shop. A notion was brewing in Gil's head, and instead of being able to shake free of it, it began to grow. What if he replaced the old woman's sad plastic daisy with a real carnation? Wouldn't that cheer up the cold, damp room she lived in?

Gil opened the umbrella and pushed through the rain to the flower shop. He pounded heavily on the door until he heard Mr. Ostergood struggling to open the door. "We're not open yet," the older fellow barked.

"It's me, Mr. Ostergood. Gil Hayworth. I need your help."

Eventually the door clicked open, and Mr. Ostergood stood before him in a bathrobe and slippered feet.

"Kinda early, ain't you, Gil? I ain't even finished with my bran flakes."

"I'm sorry. I want to order some flowers, maybe even one to take with me."

"One flower? You only want one flower?"

"Well, actually, I want several, but I just want one today." Gil felt like a naughty little boy. He was wishing he'd gone on to the pharmacy. "Maybe I can come back later."

"Naw, I'm here now. Let me get this straight. You want to take one flower with you. What kind of a flower do you want?"

"I kind of like that bright pink carnation there." He pointed to a vase of showy flowers in the case. "And then if you'd just put a different colored carnation out in your mailbox each morning, Monday through Friday, I'd pick it up without troubling you this early again."

The old man eyed Gil suspiciously. "Are these for Pam?" he asked, and Gil felt a sharp twinge of guilt.

"No, they aren't, but I do want a pretty bouquet for Pam too. This weather is really getting her down. Maybe you could have your helper deliver it to her office at the school later. She'd love it."

"I can do that, Gil." He wrapped the bright pink carnation in green florist's paper and handed it to Gil. "Have you got something going on the side, young man?"

Mr. Ostergood was an old gossip. It wouldn't be so good if everyone in town thought Gil was into a little hanky-panky.

"No, Mr. Ostergood, I'm just trying to use your beautiful flowers to brighten someone's day down at the old hotel."

"The old Grand? If you have a friend down there, she must be pretty moldy. Are you sure she's alive?" He slapped his leg at his own joke.

"She's alive. I'm not sure about her being moldy."

"Shall I send the bill to your house?" he grinned, waggishly, implying that Pam might see the bill.

"Sure," Gil told him. By then he'd have told Pam about the flowers, and she'd understand.

Gil tucked the carnation under his raincoat and ran for the car. He had just enough time to get to the hotel and replace the flower before he had to open the store. He'd be behind on the refill prescriptions that had been called in on the answering machine, but he'd allow more time in the future. And since he knew the old woman was out and about on the streets, he wouldn't be in her room when she was.

He pulled up close to the hotel's front door and made a mad dash through the door and up the stairs. As he pushed open the creaky door to her room, the stench of whiskey and body odor hit him full in the face. *Why hadn't the room stunk before?* he wondered. It was so foul now Gil could hardly get in and out fast enough. He pulled the white plastic flower out of the whiskey bottle and replaced it with the real pink carnation.

"There! Wonder what she'll think of that?" he said, his voice echoing through the sparsely furnished room.

He retreated hurriedly, more like a thief than a Good Samaritan, but he felt good. Everyone needs a lift sometime. *Maybe the carnation will give my Lady Rags a much-needed boost.*

Back in the car, he shook his head gloomily. "*My* Lady Rags? I actually thought *that*! Maybe I am losing my mind."

*****

The first thing Mollie saw on entering the room was the bright pink carnation, and her stomach lurched in fear. *Someone's been here again.* She wondered if it was the man in the white car. She had seen him again this morning over by the Ho Hum Café. She wasn't sure if he'd seen her, but she had recognized the car. What did he want with her? Was she going to have to leave Grayport because of him?

Mollie hated the idea of moving on, but the damp weather caused increasing aggravation to her arthritic bones, making it harder to climb up and down the hotel's steps, and now with someone lurking about, she knew she had to consider the possibility of leaving Grayport.

Duke wouldn't be happy with her if she told him that they had to leave. He might even refuse to go. He seemed pretty happy in Grayport.

In July when she and Duke had stepped off that old scow up from Portland, she'd misread the weather. It had been sunny and hot that day, and she'd heard that the Pacific Northwest had moderate climate. To her, moderate meant warmer year-round and no winter snow. She hadn't counted on moderate with too much rain.

She and Duke had been headed to Seattle until the captain of the scow said something about prostitutes being murdered in Seattle. Mollie wasn't a prostitute, but she'd been mistaken for one plenty of times, and she didn't want to be murdered by accident.

Now there was a chance that she could be murdered in the little home away from home she'd set up in the old hotel. Duke had nagged at her to stay at the Union Gospel Mission, but that was a definite *no*. Mollie couldn't explain to him why it was a no. It just was. The thought of someone preaching to her scared her to death.

She wasn't afraid of the Lord. Hadn't he carried her along this far, provided her with shelter, and made sure there was always plenty of food in those dumpsters? She knew he wouldn't approve of the whiskey she had stashed, but she used that strictly for medicinal purposes, and that meant warming her insides when the chill went too deep. He might not approve of her "borrowing" a room at the wonderful Edgemoor Hotel either, but she hoped he wouldn't deal with her too soon for that. She was planning on spending Thanksgiving there.

As she stood staring at the carnation, her raincoat dripping all over the floor, she was racked with another bout of coughing. She held her sides until the cough subsided. The cough had started soon after the intruders had forced her to flee her room without her boots. She always got sick if she didn't wear her boots—well, she didn't know if she always had, only as far back as she remembered.

She removed the raincoat and draped it over the back of the one wooden chair she had and hung her rain hat over the back of the short-legged chair.

Her eyes kept going back to the flower. Finally, she couldn't bear it any longer. She leaned over and took a long whiff. It smelled wonderful, its pungent scent going deep into her nostrils. When she realized the flower had no water, she immediately removed the carnation from the vase, pulled back the canvas, and held the vase out the window until it was full of rainwater. *Wouldn't want it to wilt while I wait for someone to attack me,* she thought.

Fully clothed, she lay down on her lumpy cot and pulled the tattered blankets around her. It was still daylight, and later she'd have to scavenge for her supper, but right now she needed to rest. She'd found another bottle of whiskey, empty except for a few swallows on the bottom, in a garbage can this morning. She drank the bottle dry, the liquor warming her belly and began to relax under the covers. As she dozed, she kept one eye on the bright pink spot in the otherwise drab, cold room.

4

Orville Ostergood was true to his word, and Gil removed the fresh carnation from the florist's deep, rectangular mailbox each morning and drove to the Grand Hotel before opening the drugstore. During his stops at the hotel to leave a fresh flower, he never found Lady Rags "at home." By the end of the first week, he'd discovered that carnations do not fade overnight, and the growing bouquet of flowers filled the stale room with a spicy fragrance. Gil had no idea what Lady Rags thought of his gift, but she hadn't removed them, which encouraged him.

The morning before Thanksgiving, Gil, short on time and out of breath, raced up the stairs at the hotel and found the room tidier than usual. The whiskey bottle holding the carnations had been replaced with a tall, fat vase made of crinkly green glass. Some of its fluted edges were broken off, evidence that the vase had been retrieved from someone's garbage can, but it was definitely better-looking than the bottle. Gil smiled. His daily gift had been accepted after all. He hoped eventually that she'd accept him enough to talk to him. He wanted desperately to know where she'd come from and how she'd ended up on the streets of Grayport. Gil suspected that there was more to her story than the usual "down-and-out" tale. Gil left the hotel and drove straight to the drugstore to begin a busy day.

With the next day being a holiday, more customers would be anxious to get their prescriptions filled in case they ran out of medication. Some of them would be back on Friday on drugstore business, but it would never occur to them to wait until Friday to refill a prescription.

Harv wandered into the store in the late afternoon, and after offering his witticism to two of Gil's clerks, he found his way to the pharmacy where several customers stood waiting for their prescriptions.

"Hey, the place looks good. Is it Thanksgiving or Christmas?" he laughed, heartily.

Gil knew that he was referring to the Christmas decorations that his clerks had recently displayed from one end of the store to the other. Gil didn't like squeezing Thanksgiving into a corner to make room for Christmas, but he had to keep up with the other merchants.

"Looks like you're busy," he told Jeanne, the bright, cheery young A-tech that Gil had trained himself.

She nodded as she kept counting tablets and filling bottles. Jeanne was married with a two-year-old son, but on busy days, she came in to help Gil out.

"Yeah, we've really been busy," Gil told his friend. He dumped more pills out into a tray to count. "Do you need your pills refilled?"

"Naw, I'll wait 'til the first of the week. I just wanted to wish you and the gals a Happy Thanksgiving."

"Thanks, Harv. Same to you."

"I was also wondering how things are going with you and your girlfriend?" Gil saw Jeanne look up, surprised. He could have cheerfully throttled Harv.

"Nothing much. I've been too busy helping Pam get ready for Thanksgiving guests to give her much thought," he lied. He was not going to discuss Lady Rags with anyone right now.

"Just thought maybe she was coming to your house for Thanksgiving dinner," he laughed, loudly.

"Now wouldn't Pam and her whole family love that?"

Gil knew that Jeanne was twitching with curiosity so as soon as Harv left, he explained about the bag lady.

"Oh, I've seen her in the alley right behind the store a couple of times," she told him. "She was trying to get into our dumpster, but I shooed her away."

"What could she possibly find in our dumpster?" Gil wondered. "There's nothing in there but paper and boxes."

"Well, the last time I saw her out there she was trying to reach a set of old outdated bath products that Marie had thrown out. Marie

27

said it had been in the store so long no one even bought it when it was on sale."

Gil chuckled. "Did she get it? Do you know?"

"Not while I was watching. I closed the lid and told her to scram."

Gil smiled to himself. What would she want with bath powder? There's no place to take a bath at the Grand Hotel, and from the stench in her room, Lady Rags's old bones hadn't seen soap and water for quite some time.

As soon as Gil closed the store at six o'clock, against his better judgment because he knew he should be hurrying home to help Pam get ready for the next day, he made his routine loop through Grayport's business district, hoping to spot Lady Rags. It had not rained now for several days, and pedestrians were enjoying the respite even though most of them still carried umbrellas. The sun had never quite broken through the heavy clouds, but the sky had lightened enough to lift everyone's spirits. He smiled, thinking of one in particular who might be happier without rain pouring down her neck as she wandered the streets in the wee hours.

The contrast between his life and the old scavenger's life always struck Gil soundly as he drove up Broad Street hill and turned into his own driveway. While her meager possessions were stashed in a cold, dank hotel room, he had everything he could possibly want or need, including the beautiful Colonial home on the hill overlooking Grayport.

Gil had been less than enthusiastic about the two-story house with its green gambrel roof when he'd first seen it twenty years earlier. Pam loved it at first sight, and its state of disrepair had been a challenge for her. Gil had given in to Pam's arguments in favor of the house, and they had become homeowners. She had been pregnant with Boyd at the time. Gil had just bought the drugstore from his friend and mentor, Jim Hayes, and the future seemed fraught with debt.

From the time they bought the house until after Traci's birth, Pam had put her college business degree on hold so she could raise the children and restore the house. So much love went into both ventures. A child had played on a tricycle or in the playpen while Pam refinished oak furniture she'd bought at garage sales and secondhand stores. She had pushed Tim, their second son, in a stroller with Boyd tagging along beside as she shopped for floor coverings, wallpaper, kitchen, and bathroom fixtures. The process of restoring the house to her satisfaction took Pam twelve years, and Gil knew that he'd never be able to pry her loose from it. He also knew that he would never try. The white Priscilla curtains on windows throughout the colorful, braided rugs on the hardwood floors and the cozy Early American atmosphere pleased him as much as it did Pam.

Though Gil's being proprietor of his own drugstore and being a full-time pharmacist left him little time to help Pam in those early years, she hadn't seemed to mind. She was always the first to claim he was the best pharmacist in town, and, because of her, many new mothers had come to him for advice and prescriptions. Most of those families were still customers even though their children were grown.

If anything was going wrong in the Hayworth family, as it seemed to be of late, it was not just Gil's fault and his interest in Lady Rags. It was also Tim's attitude, Boyd's going off to college, Traci whining ever since she got braces, and Pam's job which she loved but it also had its moments. After all the ups and downs the Hayworth family had already come through, it couldn't fall apart now.

Gil was still reminiscing as he pulled the white Ford sedan into his own driveway and punched the garage door opener. He promised himself that he would not think about Lady Rags until Thanksgiving was over.

*****

No one in Grayport was surprised when the brief spell of dry weather suddenly changed to gale force winds that blew in off the coast during the night. Tall evergreen trees, usually so stately and serene, swayed wildly in the fifty mile an hour wind.

"I hope no one has trouble getting here in this weather," Pam said early Thanksgiving morning.

Gil had already been at the window every few minutes, checking the storm. "I hope the power stays on. We may wish we'd bought baloney in case we can't eat turkey."

"No way I'm eating baloney today." Pam laughed. "The turkey will get done. It's already been in the oven for two hours." She had been up early to stuff the large turkey and get it into the oven along with a ham and roast beef also roasting in the double ovens.

Gil busied himself putting logs in each of the fireplaces—in each of the four bedrooms upstairs, in the dining room, and in the large stone fireplace in the living room. Even if the power went out, at least the rooms would be warm.

As Gil built a fire upstairs in Traci's bedroom, he remembered how awful the damp, mildewed upstairs had smelled when they'd first bought the house.

The elderly owners had kept the unused rooms closed to save on their heat bill. Gil had complained that the rooms would never air out, but Pam had cleaned and scrubbed until the smell was only an unpleasant memory.

Ernest and Hilde Olson, Pam's parents, arrived at ten o'clock in spite of the storm, and Pam's five brothers, their wives, and children arrived in stages from their homes around Western Washington as the day progressed. Pam was thankful that none of her family lived in Eastern Washington and would have had to come over the treacherous mountain pass to get there.

The house, full of roast turkey smells, rang with laughter, and Gil enjoyed every minute of it. Being an only child, he'd often wished for a brother or sister. When he married Pam, he's been supplied with all the brothers he needed. He liked each of the brothers, but a few of the wives mystified him. Pam had laughed at him once and said not to worry. She didn't understand a couple of them herself.

Gil had been surprised when he'd been accepted so readily into the Olson family. After all, being in love with the only girl in the family brought with it some responsibilities. Since Gil had known the Olson boys all his life and one or two had even beaten up on him on the school playground, he'd been a little fearful of asking if he could marry their sister. Evidently, they had mellowed by then because they had been enthusiastic in their consent.

As he wandered through the house talking to his guests, he wondered what they'd think of him if they knew he was sending flowers to a bag lady. He realized then that he'd broken his promise to himself. It was hard not to be concerned though with a storm howling outside. Was she in out of the wind and the rain? Surely she was smart enough to protect herself on a day like today.

*****

Gil would have been surprised if he'd known where Mollie was on that Thanksgiving Day, and he would have been reassured to know she was definitely in out of the wind and the rain. She was completely oblivious to the weather outside.

Bubbles ran over the side of the bathtub in Room B12 at the fashionable Edgemoor Hotel and dissolved into the bathroom's thick, lavender shag carpet as Mollie soaked herself in the warm tub with only her weathered face protruding out of the bubbles. The bubbles came from an almost-empty bottle of dishwashing detergent that Mollie had pulled from a garbage can behind someone's home. *Thank goodness they don't recycle,* she'd thought.

Mollie had decided a trip to the Edgemoor might be feasible since it was Thanksgiving, and most people were home with families. The few that might be staying at the Edgemoor wouldn't be using "her" room on the basement floor.

She soaked and remembered her first trip to the Edgemoor Hotel not long after she and Duke had arrived in Grayport.

Curiosity about the hotel, a large chalet structure built on a hillside with hundreds of lighted windows blinking down on Grayport, had prompted Mollie to shuffle her way across town and up the hill to get a closer look. She had waited until nearly dusk on a late summer day for her trek, so by the time she arrived at the hotel, the sky was totally dark. Getting across town through the alleys had been no problem. The long climb up the steep hill had been the problem. She had hidden in the shadows more than once to allow herself time to catch her breath and to avoid being seen by a police prowl car. At the rear of the hotel, she had checked in the dumpster to see if anyone had thrown out anything she could use and was disappointed that the dumpster was nearly empty. She'd hidden in the bushes and waited.

A vapor light illumined the area behind the hotel, so Mollie had to be careful. After about an hour of listening for any activity on the lowest floor of the hotel, Mollie decided that it might be safe to look around. Drapes on several ground-floor windows were open, indicating that the rooms were vacant. Mollie found an "Employees Only" door unlocked, and she slipped quietly into the hotel. No one was around to stop her as she moved cautiously down the short hall that connected to a wider corridor. To her right and barring her way was the laundry, so she turned around and went left along the wider corridor, trying doorknobs as she went. She had once worked as a maid in a hotel in Fresno, California, and she knew all empty rooms were locked tight, mostly to keep people like her out of them, but it never hurt to try.

To her surprise, one of the knobs turned easily in her hand, and the door opened. "Praise be!" she'd thought as she'd cautiously stepped into the room, fully expecting someone to jump out and scare the wits out of her. The vapor light outside allowed enough light into the room that she could see her way to the bathroom where she checked for dead bodies in the bathtub or in the closet. That had happened to her once in Fresno, and she didn't want a repeat performance. Finding no evidence that the room was occupied, Mollie checked the lock on the door and discovered that it was broken. It locked from the inside but not from the outside. Some employee would be in big trouble when management found out about the unlocked room. Until that happened though, Mollie applauded her good fortune, and, after propping a chair against the door, just in case, she stretched out across the wide bed and slept.

On that first visit, Mollie had not been brave enough to stay long, so before daylight, she'd crept out of the hotel and made her way back down to Grayport and across town to the Old Grand. On her second visit up the hill, she'd been brave enough to pull the drapes and turn on the lights. Then it had been immediately apparent why the room wasn't the pride of the hotel. It was painted a pale lavender with a darker lavender carpet. The bed was covered with a white-and-lavender spread with bold purple flowers. Mollie had grimaced but didn't know why. If purple wasn't her favorite color, it was the first inkling she'd had of that fact. Still the room was sheer heaven to her.

Her more frequent treks back to the Edgemoor had been for test purposes, and gradually, as she'd gone undetected with each visit, she'd gone from quick snoozes on the bed to actually removing her clothes and slipping naked in between the clean, fragrant sheets. She'd even braved turning the faucets on to wash herself. The day she'd finally ran water in the purple bathtub, she'd worried that the sound would be heard in the hall and someone would come to investigate. No one did. After that, Mollie relaxed and enjoyed each visit more and more. Still she was cautious. She didn't visit the Edgemoor on weekends or when she thought more people would be staying at the hotel. She had told Duke about the place and wanted him to take advantage of the room, but he argued that she was going to get into big trouble, probably wind up in jail. He wanted no part of it.

Now, as she soaked in the tub, each aching arthritic joint relishing the hot water, she tried again to remember who she was. She didn't know why she enjoyed sleeping naked or why she loved bubble baths. She also liked fried chicken, apple pie, and she knew how to play checkers. And she knew those things without ever even trying them. Other than that, her life before the hospital room in Joplin, Missouri, some forty years before, was a blank. Still the answers to all her questions eluded her. She did know that whatever made the ugly scar on her throat had also taken away her memory.

Mollie remembered that night in Joplin. She'd woke up in a hospital with a bandage around her throat. She didn't know why she was there or what had happened to her. She had panicked, borrowed someone's clothes from a locker in the room, and escaped. She had wandered the dark streets until she found herself in a railroad yard. Why she'd decided to hide in a freight car was something she'd probably never understand. But that's where she'd discovered Duke hiding in the same freight car. Their friendship hadn't come easy. Neither trusted the other. She'd thought he was going to trick her into going back to the hospital. He'd thought that she was some Kansas City gangster's girlfriend, and when they found her, they'd kill them both.

Dear, wonderful Duke. Tall, skinny, wonderful Duke. They had become friends. He had stayed with her, protecting her all these years without asking anything in return. Well, once he had tried and learned never to try that again.

Mollie chuckled. Poor Duke!

With all her daydreaming, the bath water had grown cool. She stood up carefully, knowing that if she fell in the tub, no one would find her for days.

She grabbed a large fluffy hotel towel and began drying herself. With her crooked big toe, she released the lever that sent the water gurgling down the drain. The sound always frightened her. Someone in the hall might hear. So far she'd been lucky, but she knew her good fortune would not last forever.

As she kept one ear alert for the sound of intruders, she wrapped another towel around her wet, stringy hair and stepped gingerly out of the tub. She went immediately to the wide bed, slid under the covers, and was instantly asleep.

While the wind blew through Grayport and knocked out power to most of the town, Mollie slept, oblivious to the rain that pounded against the window near her bed.

5

Dinner preparations in the large kitchen were well underway when the power went out the first time. Moans of disbelief came from all over the house—the women in the kitchen, the men watching football on the TV in the study, and from the young people upstairs who were playing video games on the TV in Tim's room. To everyone's joy, however, the power was back on in fifteen minutes. The women scurried now to get the green bean casserole, the mashed potatoes, and the candied yams finished and holding.

When it went off the second time, Hilde Olson threw up her hands, pulled the turkey out of the oven, tugged at a drumstick, and declared the bird was cooked enough to eat. Candles were lit, and no one seemed to mind the lack of electricity as they dished up, buffet style, and then found places to sit around the dining room table or the card tables that had been set up in the living room. Gil chose to sit on the fireplace hearth between two of Pam's nephews to eat. He tried not to notice how the wind slapped the rain against the windows of the house. He tried not to imagine Lady Rags struggling against the wind, scavenging for something to eat. What would she be thankful for today? Even the carnations in her room would be reminding her that others had more than she did. Gil wished he hadn't chosen to leave flowers when food would have been more logical.

The power stayed off long after dinner was finished, and, as custom had it in the Olson family, the women prepared the meal, so the men had to clean up afterward. Gil was put in charge of loading the dishwasher even though they'd have to wait for power before they turned it on. Pam's brother, Tom, scraped and rinsed them as her brother Bob gathered dirty dishes from around the house and stacked them by the sink. Ernest and Pam's other brothers hung around the kitchen, enjoying the time they could all spend together even though they were scorned for their lack of participation. There was laughter and camaraderie among the men just as the women were enjoying their chatty conversations in the living room by the fireplace.

Gil had even been grateful that Tim had left his sullenness in bed that morning and had been cheerful and talkative with all his cousins. Traci, who had worried that some relative would make fun of her braces, discovered that two of her cousins also wore braces, and her Aunt Penny sported a mouthful as well. She had relaxed noticeably as the day wore on. Boyd was his natural ebullient self, able to converse with the tiniest cousin as well as all his uncles. Gil thought that he'd make an excellent politician but was grateful that Boyd's desire was to go into journalism.

Just before dusk, during a lull in the storm, Pam's brothers packed up their families and left for their own homes. Ernest and Hilde waited until all their sons had departed before they bid farewell as well. They were anxious to return to the retirement home in Olympia before the storm hit again.

The Hayworth house was quiet. Boyd stretched out on the living room couch and promptly fell asleep. Traci was on the phone upstairs in her room, filling her friend Kari in on all the charms, or not, of her male cousins. Tim had left in his old blue Chevy supposedly to check out storm damage around town. Gil and Pam knew he was going to meet Bailey Nickerson, but neither wanted to end a pleasant day with a quarrel. Gil stretched out on the rug in front of the fireplace, and Pam snuggled down beside him.

"How often did you think about her today?" Pam asked.

Gil looked at her, surprised. "What makes you think that I did?" He looked puzzled.

"I know you, Gil. I also saw that worried look when you were checking out the storm through the windows."

"I confess. I did think about her being alone in that old hotel, cold and hungry, while we were stuffing ourselves in front of the warm fire."

"I thought about her too," Pam said.

"You did?" Her admission really surprised him.

"I even felt guilty, having such a nice time while she has nothing."

"Maybe I should have invited her to dinner." He laughed.

"I said I felt guilty but not that charitable." She leaned her head against his shoulder. "One thing for sure, if she was at the Old Grand, she never knew the power was out."

"I hope she went to the Union Gospel Mission or the Salvation Army today where she could eat and get warm." Gil thought about driving around town to see if he could spot her anywhere, but he wouldn't do that to Pam. He'd just stay here by the fire, close to her, and try not to think about the other woman.

Though the Friday after Thanksgiving was a holiday for Grayport schools. Tim's football team had one final game to end their winless season. Gil knew that his son's bad attitude didn't come from football losses. Tim looked forward to every game and never blamed any of his teammates for their poor season record. For that, Gil and Pam were grateful. His attitude toward his fellow team members encouraged them to think that there was still some good in the young man's heart. They were also thankful that Bailey Nickerson didn't play football. At least Tim still had one place that wasn't corrupted by Bailey's standards.

The wind had blown itself out, but the rain continued all day Friday. That evening, Gil and Pam huddled together in the stands watching Tim's football game being played on a muddy field. The gold-and-white uniforms of the Grayport Gulls became so mud splattered it was impossible to distinguish them from the black-and-gold uniforms of the West Haven Hawks. Near the end of the third quarter, a player went up to catch a pass, but neither team was sure who he was. Too late the Hawks realized that the player was a Grayport Gull and their efforts to tackle him were useless. Grayport fans went wild as the lanky fellow hurled himself headlong into the end zone, exhausted from his seventy-yard dash to the goal. It was a touchdown that would be talked about for months to come, maybe even for years. When the game ended, Grayport fans were jubilant. Their team had won their first game all season, six to zero.

Gil and Pam ran through the pouring rain to their car and found Traci and her friend, Kari, already there.

"Can we give Kari a ride home?" Traci asked.

It was a question Gil had heard after every ball game or school dance. Kari's parents never seemed available to retrieve their daughter. "Sure, we can do that," Gil told her.

He pulled the white sedan into post-game traffic. "I think we need to celebrate our only win of the season," he told them. "Could I interest anyone in a burger?"

"Can Kari have one too?" Traci asked.

"Sure, Kari can have one too." Out of the corner of his eye, he saw Pam laugh and shake her head. "I know," he whispered, "I'm such a wuss."

Gil drove through downtown Grayport and across the bridge into the south end of town to Ozzie's. The small In-N-Out lacked appeal for the teenagers of Grayport, but Gil thought Ozzie had the best burgers and fries in town.

As soon as their hamburgers and fries were bagged and their drinks handed through the car window, Gil pulled the car into a parking space in a dimly lit area behind Ozzie's. While the girls in the back seat ate and giggled, Gil and Pam ate in silence, listening to the rain pound the car's roof.

"Gil! Look!" Pam exclaimed. "Isn't that your old woman?"

Gil looked to where Pam pointed. A tall figure garbed in a slicker with a black rain hat pulled down over her head rummaged through the large trash bin at the rear of the building. They watched as she pulled pieces of food out, examined them under the vapor light, and popped them into her mouth.

"Gross! That makes me sick," Traci hissed from the back seat. "How can she eat that stuff?"

"I guess when you're hungry, you'll eat anything," Gil told her.

Pam watched, mortified. "Gil, buy her a hamburger or something. Don't let her eat garbage."

"I'm sure she's used to eating this way. If I try to buy her something, I'll only scare her off." He thought about the carnations. She might accept the food if she knew it was the same person giving it, but he hadn't told Pam about the carnations yet, and he couldn't explain to Pam right now, not with Traci and Kari in the car.

Traci leaned over the seat and handed Gil her burger. "Here, give her this. I'm not hungry anymore." Gil wasn't sure if Traci really wasn't hungry or if she'd had a rare moment of compassion.

Gil rewrapped the burger in the foil wrapper and opened the car door. The old woman saw him and stepped back into the shadows of the building. Gil placed the burger on top of the other food in the trash bin, hoping she'd think he was discarding it. He returned to the car and waited. When she didn't emerge from the shadows, he started the car's engine, preparing to leave.

"She took it!" Traci squealed. "I saw her."

Gil was relieved. "At least we know she had something fresher to eat tonight. She's quite a way from the Old Grand. I wonder what she's doing over here across the bridge."

"Maybe she likes Ozzie's food as much as you do." Pam laughed.

"Gee, Dad, maybe you ought to offer her a lift back to the hotel," Traci chided him.

"You people are sick," Kari said in disgust. "How can you even joke about that awful person? I feel like puking whenever I see her on the street."

"Just remember, Kari, there but for the Grace of God…," Gil told her.

"No, I would never be like her," Kari said. "I'd kill myself first."

"That might be a bit extreme. What if she's an angel in disguise? Haven't you heard about them?"

"Oh sure, we've heard that stuff in Sunday school, but I can't imagine anyone believing that smelly old thing is an angel."

Gil doubted it, too, but Kari's tone infuriated him. "Well then, if she is and you are the one being sought out, I guess you're out of luck."

"Gil!" Pam exclaimed, under her breath.

"Sorry, Kari," he apologized, knowing that her friendship was important to Traci, and he didn't want the girl mad at him.

They dropped Kari in front of her house and waited until she was inside the house before pulling away from the curb.

"I'm sorry I was nasty to Kari, Traci," Gil told his daughter.

"I don't think it occurred to her that you were being nasty," Traci said. "She was probably anxious to get into the house and tell her parents that we socialize with that old bag lady."

"We don't socialize with her for Pete's sake," Gil said.

"Maybe not, but Kari will make sure all my friends know you gave her *my* hamburger."

"She's your best friend," Pam said. "Why would she do a thing like that?"

"She always does. She's always doing something to hurt my feelings. She laughs about my braces, just like Tim."

"I didn't know that, Traci." Pam tried to comfort her daughter. "Why haven't you said something?"

"It usually blows over, especially when she needs me for something or like tonight when she needed a ride." Traci hesitated. "Besides, I feel sorry for the bag lady, and I'm glad she ate my hamburger. And, Dad," she reached over the seat and patted his shoulder, "I'll understand when you want to talk about your Lady Rags. I'm proud you want to be her friend."

Tears came to Gil's eyes, and he tried to blink them away. He had never heard so much compassion in Traci's voice. Maybe their little girl was growing up.

Pam reached over and touched his hand. "Me too," she said.

*****

Mollie's heart nearly stopped with fright when the man got out of the white car and dashed through the rain to the trash can. All she needed was for someone to spot her in a garbage can and call the police.

Mollie thought she recognized the white car as the same one that had been at the hotel and also had circled around looking for her. It made her nervous that the same man was leaving flowers in her room at the hotel. What did he want anyway?

She savored every bite of the hamburger, the juices trickling down her throat. Why would anyone waste something so good? She seldom had anything so fresh and tasty. She chuckled low in her raspy throat. *If only someone would leave somethin' besides bones at the chicken place.* Mollie had a real craving for a piece of fried chicken.

As more and more cars pulled into Ozzie's, Mollie hid deeper in the shadows. Duke had told her about Ozzie's, so she'd ventured over the bridge earlier, when it was less busy, to have a look for herself. Now she dreaded the trek back over the bridge where she would be exposed to traffic. Finally, she decided she could wait no longer. She was cold and wet, and her cough had returned with Grayport's bad weather. *Too bad it's the weekend now.* She shook her head sadly. *I could've used another good soaker bath at the Edgemoor.* She chuckled again, thinking of her joke on the Edgemoor. Besides the use of the room, Mollie had also borrowed clothing from the hotel's laundry. Hotel management was going to have a hard time explaining the disappearance of a pair of a man's wool trousers and two flannel shirts. She never took more than she needed, and she always left behind her soiled apparel. It more than likely belonged to one of the hotel's previous guests anyhow.

Mollie, the southwester keeping her head dry and rain pouring off the black slicker, was fully exposed to passing cars as she made her way across the long, draw span that arched up over the Chehalis River. As she trudged back along River Street toward the Old Grand, several carloads of loud teenagers passed her, shouting obscenities at her. Since arriving in Grayport, she hadn't been assaulted, but she knew it was always a possibility. She'd been assaulted by thugs in other places where she and Duke had stayed, but she'd never suffered any more than cuts and bruises. Mollie hated to think about worse things, like broken bones. How would she ever take care of herself if someone ever did that to her? She shivered again.

To her thinking, if she hid in the shadows, raided garbage cans while everyone else slept at night, and minded her own business, no harm would come to her. She thought of the man in the white car again. *Wish he'd mind his own business,* she thought grumpily.

6

On the Saturday afternoon following Thanksgiving, Tim Hayworth, Ron Pervis, and Kyle Kendrick were riding around Grayport in Bailey Nickerson's souped-up van looking for girls. Tim suspected that most of Grayport's nice girls their age were terrified of Bailey Nickerson and the black van with psychedelic drawings painted all over it. Tim didn't blame them. Bailey's skinhead haircut terrified almost everyone. Only Ron Pervis had followed Bailey's example and had his head shaved similarly. Tim and Kyle had managed to dodge any suggestions of getting their heads shaved. Life at home was bad enough without being lectured about that too.

Tim didn't know why he hung out with Bailey Nickerson. Maybe it was because he wanted to run his own life and be free of the obscurity of being Boyd Hayworth's little brother. Boyd was the perfect son. He maintained a four-point average all through high school. He was an excellent basketball player. He also had a good part-time job at the Standard Gas Station and more friends than Tim could count. And Boyd never had a problem getting a date. Girls seemed to love his tall, blond good looks and his friendliness. Tim loved his brother and admired him, but he was never Tim Hayworth, man unto himself. Growing up, all he'd heard was "Oh, you're Boyd's brother." With the expectation that Tim would be a carbon copy.

Being a copy was impossible. Tim was shorter, heavier, ruddier complected, and dumber. The most he could attain was a firm three-point average on his grades, and the girls he liked didn't like him, or at least they didn't act like it. And for as much as Tim loved football, it was the quarterbacks who got all the glory.

Tim knew, too, that Bailey and his friends were heavy into drugs, but so far Tim had sidestepped any invitation to become a user. He was dumb, he wasn't stupid. He knew what drugs would do to his life, and he knew what using them would do to his chances at a football scholarship for college. Tim's parents didn't trust his judgment or choices he was making and perhaps Tim had earned that lack of trust, but he did have his own code of ethics. Even Bailey Nickerson with his intimidation would never sway him from that code.

He'd made that decision the first time he'd been invited to ride around in Bailey's van.

He and his best friend, Dave Doyle, had been leaving school that day back in September when Bailey pulled up to the curb and offered them a ride. Both had refused at first but then had climbed in, more out of curiosity than anything. The black van was the talk of the school. For Tim, it felt good to be doing something repudiated by his peers and his family. This was something Boyd would never do. He had continued to hang out with Bailey and his cronies, although he did wonder at times why Bailey wanted his friendship. In fact, Bailey intimidated his other friends more than he did Tim, almost as if he was being especially patient with Tim. Dave had refused, after the first week, to be part of it, and they had gone separate ways. Tim was hurt by that. He and Dave had been friends since first grade, gone to Sunday school together, went camping together. But Dave was a bit of a nerd, and Tim knew he'd never fit in with Bailey's friends.

As they drove up and down the streets of Grayport, yelling out the windows at every girl they saw, taunting the homely ones and whistling at the prettier ones, Tim spied the bag lady pushing her cart into the alley behind the hardware store.

"Hey, there's a real woman." He laughed, pointing her out to the others.

"What is that?" Bailey roared with laughter. "I've got to see that again!" He swung the van around with tires squealing and turned into the narrow alley. He pulled as close to the woman as he could and slammed on the brakes, barely missing her with his front bumper.

"Hi, honey! You wanna ride?" Bailey yelled out the window.

Tim was immediately angry with himself. He could see the terror in the old woman's face, and her eyes darted back and forth like a frightened animal's. "C'mon, Bailey. Back up and let's get out of here," Tim insisted.

"Wait, Timmy boy. This here's a good-lookin' broad. Look at those clothes."

Tim was looking. He remembered his father telling about the raincoat and army boots. Today, along with the boots, the bag lady wore Navy pea jacket and trousers. "Leave her alone, Bailey. You're scaring her to death." Tim reached over the seat to pull Bailey away from the window, but Bailey shrugged him off, opened the door, and climbed out of the van.

"You're not afraid of me, sweetie?" He chucked her under the chin while Ron and Kyle cheered him on from inside the van. Tim watched helplessly. "You worthless old hag, what have you got in your bag?" Bailey snatched the large plastic shopping bag out of the old lady's cart and dumped the contents onto the wet pavement. The old lady stood frozen in her tracks. Bailey grabbed her and jerked her from side to side. "Is it hard to dance in army boots?" Bailey sneered.

Tim, sickened by what was happening, jumped out of the van and grabbed Bailey, pinning his arms to his side. With his more muscular body and size, he had Bailey at a disadvantage. He was able to force him away from the woman and shoved him into the side of the van. "That's all, Nickerson!" he shouted. "I'm telling you. That's all!" When he was sure that Bailey believed him, he released his hold on him. Leaning down, Tim retrieved a pair of denim overalls, some long underwear and heavy socks from the pavement and handed them to the old woman.

"Is she your girlfriend, Hayworth? Probably all you can get." Bailey smirked. Then without warning, Bailey swung at Tim's jaw but hit the bag lady instead with a glancing blow that knocked her against the brick building. She sagged to the pavement, her lip bleeding profusely. Tim had stopped Bailey's blow with his left arm, and with his right, he shoved a fist into Bailey's stomach.

The boy clutched his middle and backed off.

"Get out of here, NOW!" Tim screamed at Bailey.

"You're makin' a big mistake," Bailey threatened.

"Don't threaten me, Bailey. You can't hurt me."

"Oh, but I already have," he told him as he climbed into the van. Bailey's friends stared in disbelief as Bailey gunned the engine and roared out of the alley, leaving Tim behind.

"Here, let me help you," Tim told the old woman.

She allowed him to take her arm and pull her to a standing position. When he tried to see how badly her lip was cut, she slapped at him, wildly, forcing him away from her. She muttered something incomprehensibly as she piled her wet belongings onto her cart, stemming the flow of blood from her lip with one of the socks. Then she pushed off, heading toward the other end of the alley.

Tim watched her go, feeling helpless and ashamed for starting trouble for her. His father had been right after all. Bailey Nickerson's idea of fun could hurt people, and what had Bailey meant when he said he'd already hurt Tim? Tim tried to make sense of the remark as he walked out of the alley and toward the Ho Hum Café.

*****

Mollie left her cart at the bottom of the stairs inside the Grand Hotel. The overalls and underwear were wet now and wouldn't be much use to her until they dried out. Her disappointment at having her goods ruined was almost as great as the fear she'd experienced. After saving up three dollars in change she'd found, she'd searched through goods at the Salvation Army store, especially for the long underwear and heavier socks. The thermal underwear she'd found had been an even greater prize than she'd hoped for. Her money hadn't stretched far enough for the underwear and the socks, but the lady at the store gave them to her anyhow. She'd even thrown in the overalls in case Mollie needed them. That lady had always been good to her. Most people she'd dealt with in Grayport had been good to her—until now.

Those danged boys. She groaned to herself as she slowly climbed the stairs. *They've spoiled everything for me now.* She shivered with cold.

She had hoped earlier in the day when the sun had finally come out, that she'd finally get warm. But the temperature hadn't gone up, it had dropped to nearly freezing. Mollie really wanted to wear the extra underwear and socks. No use worrying about that now.

She gingerly climbed a few more steps. *Maybe I should find Duke and convince him we have to leave town,* she thought. *He'll be so mad at me.* But she knew there was meanness in the kid who'd taunted her, and he probably wasn't done with her yet. It had happened in other places. Grayport wasn't any different. Mean was mean no matter where you went. She was grateful to the other boy for helping her. Hard telling where'd she'd be if he hadn't stuck up for her.

When the van had first pulled into the alley, she'd been afraid they would kill her and leave her there where she wouldn't be found for days. Why was she always afraid she'd be killed and no one would find her? It was something she couldn't remember. Her biggest fear was being buried without a name. Mollie was frightened of the possibility. Tears ran down her cheeks. *Oh, I wish I knew who I was. I don't want to die without a name.* She stood on the second-floor landing and sobbed in hoarse little croaks.

Here lies Mollie. She croaked. *That's all we know, by golly.*

When the weeping had finally stopped, she went down the hall to her room, coughing hoarsely as she went. She'd had fewer bouts of coughing lately, but her chest was so constricted it was hard for her to take a deep breath. She longed for warmth and sunshine. She longed for a good bed and a few hours of sleep. She longed for the room at the Edgemoor, but it was the weekend, and she couldn't take the chance.

She lay down on her cot and pulled the quilts up tightly under her chin. Before long, she began to feel warmer, but the shivering wouldn't stop. She dabbed at her bleeding lip and tried to will her teeth to stop chattering. This room in this old hotel, where she'd thought she'd found solace, was now going to be the death of her.

She remembered the day she'd found the old hotel and discovered no other wanderers called it home. She'd had fun searching for the odds and ends to make the room more comfortable. Grayport people had helped her too. Besides the woman at the Salvation Army store, there was the man at the service station two blocks away who allowed her to use the restroom whenever she needed. Sometimes at night when he had few customers, she took time to wash up there. The man at Goodwin's Furniture Store sometimes offered the use of a chair if she wanted to watch television when they had no customers. Mollie liked television but felt guilty when she watched it. She didn't know why, but something inside told her it was bad.

Duke didn't like her living at the old hotel. He had begged her to stay at the Mission or at a woman's shelter. He'd taken a job as a janitor at the Mission, and she was afraid they'd try to find her a job too. She wasn't looking for work. She liked everything as it was. Or at least she had until now. She didn't like being bullied by teenagers.

As Mollie lay there, dabbing her lip, she focused on the bouquet on the table. It had grown quite large and was almost too much for the vase she'd found. But she had to admit it was beautiful, and the fragrance made her feel special. Finally, Mollie dozed, too tired and too achy to cope with anything else.

7

Gil threw his armload of broken limbs onto the pile in the backyard and answered the ringing, cordless phone that he'd set on the back steps.

"Dad, can you come downtown and pick me up?" Tim sounded frantic.

The request irritated Gil. He and Pam had been working outside all morning, trying to remove all the tree limbs and debris left by the storm. Tim had not been available to help. He had left the house early to meet Bailey Nickerson. Now he expected Gil to drop everything and drive downtown.

"Where's your car? Where's the Nickerson kid? Why can't he bring you home?"

"I can't explain now, Dad. Just come and get me. Your bag lady friend has been hurt, and I thought maybe you'd want to check on her."

"How did she get hurt?"

"I'll explain when you get here. But hurry. She was bleeding pretty badly when I last saw her."

"I'll be right down. Where are you?"

"I'll be in front of the Ho Hum Café, Dad."

Gil hung up and explained to Pam what Tim had said.

"Do you want to go with me?" he asked her.

She hesitated before answering. "I don't think so, Gil, but while you're washing up, I'll make a couple of turkey sandwiches for her. Maybe she'd like a slice of pumpkin pie too."

Gil felt a stab of guilt. Of course, Lady Rags would rather have food than flowers. He still hadn't told Pam about the carnations. She had appreciated the bouquet she'd received at school, but she didn't know the rest. *If I told her now, she'd wonder what kind of idiot she'd married.* Perhaps he'd better stop by Mr. Ostergood's on Monday and stop the carnations. Maybe he'd better pay the bill before Pam saw it.

With the sandwiches and pie in a paper sack and a thermos of coffee under his arm, he kissed Pam quickly and hurried to the car. She waved to him as he backed out of the driveway, and once again he suffered a stab of guilt. He was leaving Pam to do yard work while he was going off to tend to the other woman. Granted, the other woman was no threat to Pam, but still Gil wished he'd never gotten involved in the whole bag lady thing.

Tim was waiting on the curb in front of the café. He had the passenger door open and was climbing into the car before Gil had come to a full stop.

"You'd better explain fast, Tim," Gil demanded as he pulled away from the curb. "How do you know she's hurt?"

"Bailey hit her, accidentally. He was aiming at me and hit her instead." Gil opened his mouth to ask more questions, but Tim kept talking.

"We were driving around in Bailey's van, being our usual gross selves, when I spotted the old woman going into the alley. I guess I made a smart crack about her, and Bailey went berserk. He turned the van around in the middle of the street, and we went screeching into the alley."

"*You* spotted her? Why didn't you keep your mouth shut?"

"I didn't know what Bailey was going to do. None of the guys had seen her before, and I thought it was a big joke."

"And now you know it wasn't funny?" Gil was driving and looking up and down the streets, hoping to spot her somewhere in the shadows. Many of River Street's less fortunate citizens were out of their shabby rooms, enjoying the break in the weather. A few leaned against the front of the tavern while others slouched against the light poles in front of the rescue mission, enjoying their cigarettes. "I don't see her anywhere, do you? Maybe she went back to the old Grand."

"Dad, I'm really sorry." Tim could finally understand his father's concern. "When I saw how defenseless she was against Bailey, I realized she's at the mercy of everyone in Grayport. How does she survive?" Tim was remembering socks and underwear spilled out onto the damp and dirty pavement. "She must have to scrounge for everything she has."

Gil glanced over at his son, surprised but pleased by the boy's change of heart. "Why were you and Bailey fighting? You said he was aiming at you when he hit her."

"Dad, your worthless, good-for-nothing son was actually defending her."

"Tim, I never said you were worthless *or* good-for-nothing. Your attitude of late has stunk, but you have plenty of worth." Gil decided it was a good time to clear the air between himself and his son. "When you became friends with Bailey Nickerson, your behavior took a nose dive. I'm sure you know that because I think most of it was deliberate. Your mother and I have imagined the worst, not knowing if you were doing drugs or out drinking somewhere. We've tried to give you credit for having more sense than that, but sometimes when young people are influenced by their friends, good sense goes right out the window."

Tim squirmed in his seat. "I don't do drugs, Dad. Oh sure, I tried marijuana, but my conscience always bothered me when I smoked it. I kept thinking about you and Mom. Isn't that weird? I knew you'd be disappointed in me, and I really do care what you think." He kept his eyes straight ahead, staring through the windshield. "And I've been drinking. Lots! I'm not proud of myself anymore. I thought I was having a great time, until today. When Bailey took off after the old lady, I realized how stupid he was and how stupid I've been to think he was so special."

Gil and Pam had not been unaware of Tim's alcohol use. The smell of beer and his physical appearance when he returned after being with Bailey had been so obvious, but Gil had been afraid that confronting Tim would just drive a bigger wedge between them. He and Pam had both prayed for Tim. They prayed for all their children. Now he was thankful that Tim felt he could confide in him. Perhaps Tim's concern for Lady Rags was a good start in the right direction. When Tim had needed to make a choice in a critical moment, he'd made the right one. Gil was so full of pride for his tough, redheaded son right then. It was hard to fight back the tears of joy that were trying to break free at that moment.

As they neared the deserted hotel, seagulls were visible everywhere, sunning themselves on the river bank and preening as they perched on the rotted piling that jutted up out of the river behind the hotel. "Guess the gulls appreciate a nice day too," Gil remarked as he pulled into the circular driveway and parked near the front door. "You stay in the car," he told Tim, "and don't you *ever* tell your friends where the old woman lives."

"I won't, Dad, but I'm not staying in the car. I tried to help her, so maybe she'll remember me."

Gil decided that Tim might be right. He motioned him to follow. Everything was so quiet inside the building that Gil wasn't sure Lady Rags had even come back here. If she'd been hurt, she might have gone to the rescue mission or someplace where she could get help. He had no idea who she knew in Grayport or if she had any friends.

He led the way up the stairs and along the corridor to the room. He knocked gently as he pushed the door open, knowing that even a knock wouldn't stop the alarm she might be feeling if she was there and had heard them. The creaking door woke Mollie, startling her, and she stared at them from her cot, her face full of terror, her eyes darting back and forth like a trapped animal.

"Please," Gil pleaded. "We're not going to hurt you. My son is here." He pulled Tim up where the woman could see him plainly. "He told me you were hurt. We want to help you."

She shook her head violently and motioned for them to get out. A thin wailing sound seemed to emanate from her very soul.

"I don't think she can talk," Tim whispered. "She made that same sound in the alley."

Gil stepped closer to her, and she waved her arms at him frantically. "I'm not going to hurt you. Don't you understand?" Forgetting that Tim was standing close by, Gil pointed to the bright bouquet of flowers on the table. "I'm the one who brings the flowers. I wanted to brighten up your room."

She blinked in surprise. He held up the sack of sandwiches. "My wife made you some sandwiches." He shook the thermos of coffee. "And some coffee. It's good and hot."

He set the sack and thermos on the table beside the vase of carnations. She made no move to accept any of it. The deep gash on her lip had stopped bleeding and didn't look as if it needed medical attention. In fact, Gil thought that she looked pretty fit. She had made it back to her room, unaided, so Gil decided that no part of her body, which was hidden by heavy quilts, was broken.

"My name's Gil Hayworth," he told her. "No relation to the movie star." He chuckled, wondering if she even knew who Rita Hayworth was. "And this is my son, Tim. Remember him? He was afraid you were hurt and thought we should check on you."

Gil thought the woman had relaxed a little, but she still gripped the blankets tightly under her chin. The terror had been replaced with something else, perhaps anxiety. She clearly wanted to be rid of them.

"I'd like to talk to you sometime, maybe ask you some questions. We could meet at the Mission if you wanted to," he suggested.

He wasn't sure if it was the mention of the Mission or about asking her questions, but she jerked her head violently again, motioning for them to leave. As her determination to get rid of them increased, she tried to raise her voice, but all they heard was a hoarse, grating "Git!"

Tim backed toward the door, tugging at Gil's coat. "Let's go, Dad, before she has a heart attack or stroke or something."

"Enjoy the food," Gil said to her as he backed toward the door. "Maybe I should leave my phone number in case you ever want to get in touch with me." He grabbed the paper sack off the table and hastily scribbled his home number and the drugstore's number across it. He knew it was a useless gesture, but at least he'd made contact. Now the rest was up to her.

As they left the hotel, Gil spotted the dilapidated stroller with its bag of damp cargo at the base of the stairway. He picked it up, ran back up the steps, and deposited it just outside her door.

"There!" he said, more to himself than anybody. "Maybe that'll save you some steps."

Gil and Tim were back in the car, driving along River Street, before Tim spoke. "Flowers, huh?" There was no humor in the remark.

Gil felt the sting. "Yes."

"Does Mom know?"

"What difference does it make? It's not exactly a romantic involvement, you know."

"But, Dad...to send her flowers?" Tim seemed totally disconcerted by his father's behavior. "And Mom calls *me* a dork!"

*****

Mollie waited until the hotel was quiet again before she pushed away the blankets and sat up on her cot. Every bone in her body ached, but she managed to stand up. She moved heavily to the door and checked the hallway, noting that her cart was just outside the door.

Talk about scarin' someone to death, she thought to herself. *I thought for sure they'd come to finish me off.*

Mollie sat down at the table and opened the brown bag, examining the scribbled phone numbers as she did so. She guessed that one of the numbers was for the drugstore where she'd seen the white car parked. She had no intention of calling either number, but she was glad to know who he was and that he meant her no harm. And the young man had helped her when that thug had attacked her.

She dumped the two sandwiches and a foil-wrapped packet out of the sack and onto the table. She opened one of the sandwiches and sniffed, satisfied that it really was a turkey sandwich. As she sank her teeth into it, she swooned with ecstasy. She ate slowly, chewing each bite until all the flavor was gone. She hoped that her stomach got as much pleasure from the food as her tongue was having.

After finishing the first sandwich, Mollie opened the foil-wrapped packet and discovered the slice of pumpkin pie. Her eyes filled with tears that overflowed down her rough cheeks. She hadn't had a piece of pie since they'd left California. Though apple was her favorite, pumpkin always did nicely in a pinch.

She rechecked the bag, making sure there weren't *two* pieces of pie, and then wadding the bag and tossing it into the corner, she began to eat slowly and deliberately, stretching her enjoyment for as long as possible. She poured the hot coffee into one of her own plastic cups, added some whiskey from a bottle she had stashed away in a box of old clothes, and slurped it heartily. The cut on her lip was tender and tried to break open again, but Mollie didn't care. The pleasure she gained from the food far outweighed the pain.

It suddenly occurred to her that they might be trying to poison her. She clutched at her throat and then shrugged it off. *Too late now,* she told herself. *If I'm goin' to die from this food, I'm goin' to die a very happy person.*

8

Grayport shivered under blue skies and cloudless days for the entire first week in December when the temperature plummeted from forty degrees to fourteen overnight. The wind chill factor fell well below zero. Pipes froze and burst, furnaces gave out from undue stress, and fire sirens were heard throughout the day as wood stoves were stoked beyond their limits and chimney fires erupted.

Gil worried about Lady Rags. She had disappeared. When he'd stopped by the hotel on the first of the bitterly cold mornings, he'd expected her to be out on her routine scavenger hunt for food, but there were no signs that she'd been in the room at all. The second morning he checked, he found the carnations frozen in a vase of ice. His concern grew. Had she finally sought help from the Union Gospel Mission? Gil hoped that she had. No one could survive outside in the subfreezing temperatures for long.

On his way to the drugstore that morning, he stopped at Ostergood's and cancelled his daily carnation order. It had been a silly gesture from the beginning, but he still hoped the flowers had brought some cheer into the old woman's life.

After a week of driving through narrow alleys and up and down River Street, looking for her, Gil feared the worst, that she would be found frozen to death in an obscure corner of an old building somewhere. On two different days, he'd stopped in early at the Union Gospel Mission and saw no sign of her among the food recipients.

Toward the end of the second week in December, Gil left the drugstore in midafternoon, determined to find the old woman one way or another. He drove to the Grayport Police Station and parked near the fountain that only three weeks ago had been shooting water up in every direction but now was frozen solid. Inside the station, a young woman in uniform directed him to the police chief's office.

"Gil," Fred Burgess said as he stood up to shake Gil's hand. "How the heck are you? I hope there's no problem at the store."

"No, nothing like that. We haven't even had a broken pipe... knock wood," and Gil made a fist and knocked on his own head.

"You're lucky," Chief Burgess told him. "We've had a chimney fire at our house, and we've had broken pipes here at the station. The cold snap surprised us before we got the fountain shut down, so we've had some problems with it. I'm hoping it warms up again pretty soon. Wearing all this long underwear is uncomfortable." Gil laughed in agreement. "What can I do for you, Gil?"

"I'm wondering if you know what's happened to the old woman who has been holing up in the Grand Hotel."

"Mollie? How do you know Mollie?"

"Is that her name? I just call her Lady Rags."

"I never thought much about her being a lady," the chief chuckled. "She does wear some crazy outfits though. My officers have something new to report on her clothes every time they come off duty."

"Has anyone seen her lately?"

"I'm sorry, Gil. No one has reported seeing her around town for a couple of weeks. When she and her friend first came to town, my officers kept a pretty close watch on both of them, but they never caused any problems."

"There are two of them?"

"Her friend is an old guy named Duke who works at the Mission. He's a janitor there, I think. He's still there. I just saw him a few days ago."

"I wonder why she's always alone then."

"Who knows? We charged her with vagrancy once just so she'd know we were keeping track of her, but my officers tend to ignore her. She's not hurting anyone, and she's fairly safe here in Grayport. What's your interest, Gil?"

"I've been concerned about her for a couple of months and have tried to keep tabs on her myself. I know that she had a run-in with some teenage boys awhile back, Bailey Nickerson for one and my son too."

"Tim? So he *is* running with Bailey Nickerson?"

"He was, against our wishes, but we couldn't talk him out of it. But he isn't now. How did you know?"

"Tim's name was mentioned when we talked to the girlfriend of one of the guys. She works in one of the drugstores that had some drugs missing. She said we should check out Tim. She said she believed he was the guilty one."

Gil couldn't believe his ears. "And do you need to talk to Tim?"

"No. The girl admitted later that she didn't know who had stolen the drugs. Have you had any missing drugs at your pharmacy?"

"No, and we keep good count. Tim may do some dumb things now and then, but I don't think he'd ever be that dumb."

"I didn't think so either, Gil, so don't worry about it. But we are keeping an eye on the Nickerson kid and his friends."

"Maybe that's why Bailey was so interested in having Tim for a friend. We did wonder about that since last year he totally ignored Tim. Even Tim made mention of that fact."

"Be glad Tim is staying clear of that bunch. They may be going to jail one of these days soon."

Gil turned to leave.

"Sorry I wasn't much help with your Lady Rags," the chief said. "If we locate her, we'll let you know, but I think she's left town."

"Thanks. I'd appreciate any information you can give me."

As Gil got back into his car, he repeated her name again to himself.

Mollie. It was good to finally be able to call her something besides Lady Rags. "Mollie" had accepted the flowers. "Mollie" had eaten Pam's sandwiches, or at least he thought she had. When he'd returned to her room at the hotel the following Monday morning after Thanksgiving, he'd found the empty paper sack, the one with the phone numbers, wadded up and tossed into a corner. The empty thermos bottle had been on the table, so he'd retrieved it. There had been no sign of the pumpkin pie or leftover sandwiches. And now Mollie was gone.

Gil knew the pharmacy was in good hands until closing time, so he decided not to return to the drugstore immediately. He drove to River Street and parked in front of the Union Gospel Mission. Several men leaned against the building, close to the entrance, smoking cigarettes. They spoke to Gil as he approached, and he recognized several of them as being his customers at the drugstore. Though he didn't sell cigarettes at his store, many of them were welfare prescription customers or just stopped in for aspirin, corn plasters, or for a cold drink out of the pop machine.

Inside the Mission, Gil was surprised at the number of men who sat around a long table in the large dining room. Though he knew jobs were scarce on the harbor, he hadn't realized that so many men were down on their luck.

Perhaps the cold weather had brought more of them inside, off the streets.

Clay Morgan, the Mission's director, greeted him just inside the door and motioned him inside his small office.

"Where did they all come from?" Gil asked as he sat down in a squeaky chair in front of Clay's desk.

"It's a sign of the times, Gil. That and the extremely cold weather. We usually have ten to twenty regulars in here to eat every night, but in the last few months, that number has increased to forty or more, including women and children."

"You say you have women here now?" Gil felt encouraged. "How about one named Mollie who wears green rubber boots?"

"I know who Mollie is, but she won't step foot inside this place. Her friend, Duke, works here, and he's tried to talk her into, at least, eating with us, but she refuses. Why the interest, Gil?"

"I don't really know. I saw her for the first time one morning on my way to the drugstore, and her appearance shocked me so much I couldn't get her out of my mind. Where did she come from? Do you know?"

"No, I don't, but Duke would. They came to Grayport on the same old scow, and I know he keeps in touch with her." Clay stood up and motioned for Gil to follow. "Come on. We'll see if Duke is around somewhere. He's pretty tight-lipped about everything most of the time, but he might talk to you."

Gil followed Clay to a cluster of men at the big table in the dining room, but Duke wasn't in the group. One of them, however, pointed to the enclosed back stairs where one lonely man sat, near the top, staring out the window at the darkening, cloudless sky.

"Duke?" the director said as he approached the base of the stairs. "This is Gil Hayworth. He'd like to talk to you about Mollie if you don't mind."

The thin man with stringy gray hair turned his head and looked sleepily at Gil. His face of gray stubble hadn't seen a razor for several days. The heavy wool sweater he wore over plaid polyester trousers was moth-eaten and frayed at the cuffs. "Why you nosin' around about Mollie?" he asked, raising his bushy eyebrows.

"Mollie isn't at the Grand Hotel anymore. I thought maybe you would know if she was safe somewhere else."

"You a cop or somethin'?"

"No, actually I own the pharmacy over on Main Street. Maybe you've been in there."

"How do you know Mollie? Is she yer customer?"

"No, I'm just concerned about her." Gil was hard put to explain just why he *was* interested in the old woman. "She hasn't been at the hotel for a couple of weeks."

"You the one that sends flowers?"

"Then you have talked to Mollie." Gil felt a sense of relief knowing that Mollie really did have a friend who might be keeping her out of harm's way. "Listen, Duke, I don't mean to bring trouble to your friend, and I think she knows that."

"She don't like people prowlin' 'round her place."

"I wasn't prowling. I was checking on her. The flowers were to brighten her days a little."

"Are you sure you ain't from Missouri?"

"Me?" Gil was puzzled. "Why would I be from Missouri? Is that where Mollie's from, Duke?"

"Mebbe she is. Mebbe she isn't. Just thought mebbe that's why you were so interested."

Duke's slow, deliberate speech was exasperating to Gil. He wanted information, and he didn't want to drag it out of the man.

"Look, Duke, Mollie could freeze in this weather. If you can assure me that she's safe, I'll be on my way."

"Mollie's tough. She ain't goin' to freeze."

"Maybe she isn't as tough as you think. Did you know some kid beat up on her awhile back? Cut her lip open bad."

Duke stared at Gil in disbelief. Obviously he hadn't known. Tears filled his faded blue eyes. "She'll be okay," he said, shaking his head. "She'll be okay."

Gil could see that he wasn't getting anything more out of Duke. "If I come back sometime, will you tell me about Mollie?"

"Mebbe," was all he would say.

Gil was distraught as he left the Mission. He drove back to the drugstore but saw that the lights were out, and it was locked up tight. Thankful that his A-tech knew how to handle the closing procedure, he drove straight home.

Pam sensed Gil's short temper and made an effort to keep the conversation light as she put the finishing touches on dinner and, with Traci's help, set the food on the table. Boyd and Tim were both home, and for once they all managed to eat together without bickering.

Tim had been easier to live with since he'd quit running with Bailey Nickerson, and he no longer teased Traci about her braces. And, it seems, someone besides her father thought Traci was as pretty with braces as she was without. "The most wonderful boy in the eighth grade," according to Traci, had asked her to the school's Christmas dance. Her sagging spirits were suddenly soaring. Boyd, too, was in good spirits. His college classes were going well, his hours at the service station were few but steady during the winter, and he looked forward to a promising season on the basketball team.

Gil was suddenly aware of how thankful he was for his family. He looked around the table at each of them, listening as they told of the day's events. The events that he related were about customers or happenings in the drugstore, not about his inquiries into Mollie's whereabouts. He didn't want to put a damper on everyone's high spirits.

Just as they were finishing dinner, Dave Doyle came in the back door. "Anybody home?" he said as he stuck his head around the door.

Gil was also thankful for Dave's return and his friendship with Tim. The young man had been at their house almost every night just as he had been in years past, and both he and Tim had managed to get dates with their favorite girls. Tim was dating the popular Cathy Southern, and Traci no longer chided him about that.

Tim got up from the table, preparing to leave with Dave.

"Where's Bailey Nickerson these days?" Gil asked, hating to bring up the subject but needing to know.

"Around town, I guess," Tim said. "He's been skipping school lately."

"Bet he's griped that you don't hang out with him anymore. Did you ever wonder if he befriended you because of our drugstore and an easy way to gain access?"

"Probably so, Dad. He's bad news. Evidently, someone has provided him with drugs from the other drugstores. Ours was probably next. And since the day he scared your Lady Rags to death, Bailey assaulted a man at the movies just because he thought the man had pushed in front of him. Dave was there and heard Bailey tell the man he'd get him later. And the man believed him. He just intimidates everybody."

"He wouldn't go after Mollie again, would he?" Tim looked at him, puzzled. "Oh," Gil explained, "I found out today that her name is Mollie." He explained to his family about his visit to the police chief and to the Mission. "The old fellow at the Mission thinks Mollie is from Missouri."

"He thinks?" Pam asked. "He doesn't know?"

"Evidently not. He didn't know about Mollie's encounter with Bailey, so maybe he'll talk to her and she'll be more willing to talk to me next time."

"Don't worry about Bailey, Dad," Tim told him. "I doubt if he's the reason Mollie has disappeared. I've seen him around town pursuing other interest. Maybe Mollie's holed up somewhere warmer than the Grand Hotel."

"I hope you're right. I just wish I knew where."

9

Gil returned to the Mission the following evening and was disappointed when Duke was not among the men who were filling the seats for the nightly church service. Clay Morgan encouraged Gil to stay for the service, thinking Duke might return. Gil slid into the back pew and watched the door while he listened to the words of Grayport's Baptist minister, whose turn it was to provide the service that evening. Several churches provided services and enough food for the suppers. Pam had provided food many times when it was their own church's turn on the calendar.

Despite the lack of funds that plagued the Mission, it was still a clean, pleasant refuge for those who had no other place to go. There was always food available for the hungry and spiritual food for the soul. Many of those who sat through the evening service did so because they were required to listen to a sermon if they wanted to eat. Many also listened intently, craving the peace that God alone could give their souls.

Before the service ended, the street door opened, and Duke appeared. Gil's relief was so great he heaved a sigh of relief that could be heard throughout the small sanctuary. The tall, lanky man slid into the seat next to Gil and bowed his head for the closing prayer. Then Gil followed him to the dining room where supper was being served.

Gil sat down across from Duke. "You've seen her, haven't you?"

Duke stuck a fork into the tuna noodle casserole on his plate and nodded. "Yep," he said.

"Is she all right?"

"Yep."

Gil persisted, his irritation mounting. "I wish you'd talk to me."

"Mollie likes you. Mebbe you can help her."

Gil was surprised but glad. "How can I help her?"

Duke hesitated again, choosing his words carefully. Gil wondered if he'd had a speech problem sometime in his life. "She don't know who she is," Duke explained.

"You asked me if I was from Missouri. You must know that much about her."

"I found her in Joplin, Missouri," he said, slowly and carefully. "Her and I hopped the same freight train there. I could tell she knew nothin' about ridin' freights. She was pretty scared."

"And you didn't know her before that?"

"Nope. She just showed up, and we've been travelin' together ever since. I worry because she's all alone. I look out for her."

"Does she have amnesia?" Gil could tell by Duke's expression that he was unfamiliar with the word. "Can she remember anything?"

"Nope. Might have somethin' to do with the ugly scar on her neck. Looks like someone tried to cut her head off. She's always nervous, scared-like, and she don't know why."

Duke paused and took several bites of casserole. Gil waited. He knew the information he was searching for was inside Duke's head. It was just slow in coming out.

"She remembers wakin' up in a hospital in Joplin and bein' scared out of her wits," Duke continued. "She didn't know why she was there, and she didn't know why her throat was bandaged. She found a dress there in the room that didn't fit, but she put it on. It was a gawsh-awful lookin' thing. She was wearin' it when she climbed into that freight car where I was."

Gil thought he saw a smile playing at the corners of Duke's mouth as he remembered back. "She was a sight," Duke said. "That baggy dress, her blond hair lookin' like she'd just been in a tornado, and that bloody bandage wrapped 'round her neck."

Duke took several more bites of casserole and slurped down half of his glass of milk. "I wasn't happy about her bein' on the train with me. She kept bein' sick and throwin' up, and I knew she was goin' to get us caught. She was scared of me, so I let her be. We were in Amarillo, Texas, before I figured out she couldn't talk. She was such a skinny little thing. I tried to get her to eat, but she kept pushin' me away."

"How old do you think she is, Duke?"

"Now? Late sixties, mebbe." Gil could tell that Duke was remembering more and more by the smile that crinkled his watery blue eyes. "When she first climbed on that train, I thought the Lord had rewarded me for somethin'. I hadn't had a woman in a while, and I could see that this one would be purty if she were fixed up. I guessed her to be about thirty-five, some younger than me. But she made those gawsh-awful gurglin' noises in her throat, and that's when I figgered I'd best stay away from her."

Gil remembered the scared eyes and the sounds Mollie had made when he and Tim went into her room at the old Grand. "Do you know if she has family anywhere?" Gil's imagination was going wild. What if someone had been looking for her all these years?

"Don't know. After we left Amarillo, she let me talk to her, and I'd tell her words hopin' somethin' would jar her thinkin'. Nothin' did. She'd just sit and cry."

"How did she talk to you?"

"Waved her hands around a lot, and when I couldn't figger it out, she'd try to whisper, but that hurt her throat. One time, she let me see where someone had tried to slit her throat. It made me sick to look at it. Since she didn't know her own name, I called her Mollie. I figgered someone as purty as she was, she might have been a Kansas City gangster's moll, and he'd been mad enough at her to want her dead."

Gil shivered involuntarily. It was a gruesome possibility. "Is that why you thought I was from Missouri? You thought I was after her?"

"Yep. She's always afraid of strangers. But she ain't scared of you. Mebbe it's some sort of sixth sense, but she says she trusts you."

"I'd like to talk to her Duke. Can't you tell me where she is?"

"Nope. She's safe. That's all."

"Maybe I can help her find out who she is. You said she wanted to know."

"It scares her. They may try to kill her again." Duke jabbed his fork into a piece of chocolate cake that had been set before him.

Gil doubted that anyone would still be looking for her to kill her after all these years, but she might have family somewhere that never knew what happened to her. Gil stood up and prepared to leave. "Thanks for talking to me, Duke."

Duke stopped chewing. "Mebbe you can help her without her knowin' it," he said.

Gil understood. Duke would not betray his friend, but he wasn't willing for Mollie to be alone if she had family somewhere.

"I'll be careful, Duke, in looking for information. I won't let anyone hurt her again."

Duke nodded and went back to eating his cake. Gil left the Mission feeling sad and excited at the same time. Mollie *did* have a mysterious past just as Gil had suspected all along. Now he was going to make it his business to find out what it was.

*****

At the drugstore the next morning, Gil busied himself with fill-ing prescriptions and tried to keep his mind on business, but his conversation with Duke kept coming to mind. The only positive information he had was that Mollie had been in a hospital in Joplin, Missouri, but that didn't mean she was from Missouri. Gil was not a computer genius, so he didn't know where to begin his search. Boyd or Tim could help him find information on the Internet, but would hospitals have information that went back forty years, and would they give it out if they did have it? He doubted it.

Gil's thoughts were interrupted when he heard Harv bantering back and forth with the clerks as he made his way to the back of the store. "This place makes me feel good when I come in. It's so Christmassy," he effused.

"That could be because it's Christmas." Gil laughed. But Gil knew what Harv meant. When he opened the front door in the mornings and saw the lighted garlands and shiny stars hanging from the ceiling over the merchandise, his spirits always seem to lift. He loved Christmas as much as any kid and hated to see it come and go so fast, leaving dreary, rain-soaked January in its wake.

"I came to get my pills," Harv said. "Can't be without my blood pressure pills at this time of the year. When I see the bills Ellie's racking up, I think maybe I should be doubling up on the pills."

"No need to do that," Gil told him. "I'm sure Ellie's got everything under control."

"You're right about that. I have absolutely *no* control." Harv gestured widely and guffawed. "Seriously though, does everyone have to take pills this time of the year? There's too much to do and not enough time to do it."

Gil understood that perfectly. The schedule at the Hayworth house had been total chaos lately. Traci had two rehearsals a week for a Christmas musical at school, and she was also practicing for the church's nativity pageant. She was always being dropped off or picked up somewhere. Boyd had somewhere to go, usually basketball practice, but never at a time when he could chauffeur Traci. So Tim, who never volunteered for school programs or the church nativity pageant, was enlisted as official taxi driver plus supervisor of tasks at home that needed to be completed. Gil was amazed that Tim didn't complain. He seemed to like being the family coordinator, or "puller-together-of-loose-ends" as Tim called it.

Pam squeezed in some Christmas shopping between her longer hours at the elementary school. The season added more work for the teachers, so Pam helped out on art projects, room decorations, and playground supervisor whenever she could. Gil had promised himself that he'd help Pam during the holidays. Now, anxious to start tracing Mollie's past, he would have to keep his promise to Pam first and think about Mollie second. Mollie could even wait until after the holidays now that Duke had assured him that she was warm and safe somewhere in Grayport.

Still, it wouldn't hurt to ask. "Harv, whatever happened to that guy that worked for the Register, the one from the Midwest?"

"You mean Keith Weldon? He left us and went to the *Post-Intelligencer* in Seattle. Thought the weather was better there than on the harbor."

"I wonder if he's still there."

"Why would you wonder about him?" Harv was openly inquisitive. "What are you up to now?"

"I'm not *up* to anything, Harv. I was just asking about the guy."

"Must have something to do with the old bag lady. I haven't heard mention of her for a while, so I thought maybe you'd given up on her. I should have known better."

"I talked to a friend of hers who works at the Mission, and he says she's from the Midwest, maybe Missouri, and she can't remember who she is."

"Is that why you think Keith could help you? The Midwest is a pretty big place, Gil, and unless she made the newspapers, how would Keith know anything? He came from St. Louis, worked at a newspaper back there."

"I know it's a long shot, but I thought he might just know who to contact to get information on crime victims. Mollie had been in a hospital in Joplin, Missouri. Someone had unsuccessfully tried to cut her throat. Surely the hospital would have some information on that sort of thing."

Harv nodded in agreement. "You'd think so," he agreed. "You have been a busy fellow, haven't you? Let me contact the PI and see if Weldon still works for them. If not, they'll know where he went."

"Thanks, Harv. I just feel like she needs help, and she isn't getting it."

"Not a problem. However, I do think you missed your calling. Instead of a pharmacist, you should have been a reporter. You're just nosy enough to really get into a story."

Gil hadn't expected to hear from Harv again for a few days so was surprised when he came back into the store later that afternoon. "Guess what I found out? Keith Weldon didn't like Seattle any better than he liked us, so he went back to St. Louis. He works at the *St. Louis Post-Dispatch*."

"Harv, I didn't expect you to get on this so quick."

"It wasn't too tough, Gil. I just called someone I knew." He slid a piece of paper over the prescription counter to Gil. "Here's his address and phone number, but you can e-mail him too. The email address is on there too."

Gil looked at the paper and slid it into his pharmacy coat pocket. "I don't do e-mail. The only computer I try to understand is this one right here with pharmacy information. The rest is way over my head."

"Well, you should get one of those kids to teach you on your home computer. I always knew they were smarter than their old man." He laughed, loudly. "Well, I'd better get back to work. Good luck on your search. Stay out of trouble with Pam."

"Thanks, Harv. I'll try."

After Harv left the store, Gil pulled the small piece of paper from his pocket. Should he try the phone number now or wait to do it from home this evening? He glanced at the long line of prescription slips needing attention and saw how busy Jeanne was. He slipped the paper back into his pocket and picked up the next prescription slip in the long line.

10

Mollie knew she had stayed too long at the Edgemoor, and there was a good chance she'd be found, but it felt good to be warm. As she lay naked in the queen bed, the lilac comforter pulled up tightly under her chin, she sipped the remains from a bottle of bourbon and felt the warmth sooth her tight, aching chest. She hardly coughed at all now. She wished she could. It might ease the pain from the congestion she'd been battling.

It had only taken one bitterly cold night at the Grand Hotel to convince Mollie that she'd better seek shelter elsewhere. Wearing two pair of long underwear and all three pair of men's woolen socks inside her green boots did little to prevent the chill that went to her bones. Mollie suspected that much of the chill came from whatever made her chest ache, but no matter, she wasn't going to find a doctor to find out.

Mollie had trudged across town and up the hill to the Edgemoor before daylight the second day after the temperature dropped below freezing and after she'd discovered her bouquet was frozen solid. She didn't want to meet the same fate.

The going had been difficult. The wind had whipped around her, and frozen tree limbs had snapped at her. The cold, dry air made the streets so dry she hadn't worried about slipping on ice. There wasn't any. Still, when she'd arrived at the Edgemoor, she'd been exhausted.

When she'd tried the faulty lock on her special room, the door had opened quietly. "Thank you, Lord," she'd murmured. After bracing the door with a chair, she had immediately thrown herself on the bed, fully clothed, and fell asleep. When she woke up, she wasn't sure how long she'd been asleep, but it was dark, and the moon was high in the sky. She'd slept all day and into the night again.

She'd stripped and bathed, using the same bar of the hotel's small complimentary soaps she'd used previously and the same towels that she's used before and hung back on the towel rack in the bathroom. After her nice soaker bath, she'd climbed back under the covers and slept some more. She had lost all track of time.

Twice in those next days, hunger had sent her into the hall looking for food. On her first trip out of the room, she'd found warm dinner rolls in the unoccupied kitchen. On the second trip, she'd found a bowl of fresh fruit, a loaf of bread, and a decanter of wine on a tray setting on a cart in the lower hall. Mollie had pushed cart and all into her room and locked the door behind her, snickering at the good trick she'd played on the people who worked in the hotel. No great alarm ever went up after she stole things, so she helped herself to whatever she thought she needed.

When Duke showed up at her door and tapped out their signal—three knocks and a scrape—he didn't think her escapades were so funny. He always worried that she'd be caught and hauled off to jail. Mollie had tried to reassure him that she knew what she was doing. As long as the room was unused and the hotel was unaware of the broken lock, she was perfectly safe. She tried to be as quiet as possible, and she never turned on the television set in the room. She knew though that she'd never convince him.

"Your friend in the white car showed up at the Mission," he told her. "He was askin' all sorts of questions 'bout you. I didn't know how much you wanted him to know."

Mollie's hands and fingers moved rapidly as she signed her answer. "Tell him what he wants to know," she signed. "I trust him. He's been good to me."

"How long you goin' to stay here this time? You've already been here nearly two weeks."

Mollie hadn't realized it had been that long. "Don't know," she signed. "It's still too cold for me outside, so I'll stay a little longer." She pounded her chest with her fist and coughed. "This is getting worse."

"Mebbe you need a doctor." Duke knew what her reaction would be when he said it. Always when he mentioned doctors, hospitals, nurses, anyone in the medical profession, Mollie went into a tizzy. He guessed it had something to do with the hospital in Joplin, Missouri. Nothing was different this time. She started shaking all over and making wild noises.

"Mollie! Be quiet! Someone will hear you," he said, trying to calm her down. "Just forget I said it."

Mollie started to cough, a racking painful cough that made Duke hurt just to listen to her. "Mebbe I can find some medicine for you. I'll try."

Mollie nodded, grateful for his help and his friendship. Finally, when the coughing stopped, she reached for the telephone and handed it to Duke. "Call room service," she signed, "and order us some steaks."

"Mollie, I cain't do that!" he told her, panic in his voice.

"Just do it," she signed angrily. "I'm hungry and next time you come, bring some fried chicken."

Duke knew how much she liked chicken, and he wished he'd brought some this time. But he did as she asked and took the phone, knowing full well that if room service showed up, Mollie's use of the room was doomed. Mollie, on the other hand, was sure the room service people didn't know who was registered to which room, so they'd never know the difference.

When the young man in a blue jacket and white pants knocked on the door, Duke opened the door for him. When the young man uncovered the plates on the cart and the aroma filled their nostrils, Duke decided he didn't care if Mollie was right or wrong, he was going to eat now and pay for his crime later. He pulled the last dollar bill from his worn pants pocket and handed it to the young man.

They ate in silence, each savoring the tasty steak, the baked potato, and the crisp green salad. Though Duke enjoyed every bite, he still waited for someone to break down the door and haul them both away.

Later, after Duke had gone back to the Mission, Mollie stretched out in the bed once again. She chuckled to herself. Duke had been nervous about ordering the meals, but he had enjoyed every bite. It was her way of thanking him for being her friend all these years. He'd looked out for her all the way from Missouri to California. He's the one who dubbed her Mollie. He thought she was somehow mixed up with gangsters. Mollie didn't know if she had been or not. For sure, someone hadn't liked her much and slashed her throat to prove it.

When they'd arrived in Fresno, California, all those years ago, Duke got a room for them and found himself a janitor's job. He was a good worker and never had any problem finding or keeping a job. He also found someone who was willing to try her as a waitress. Even though she couldn't talk, they thought she was pretty enough and quick enough to handle the job. Most customers had understood her handicap and were very kind. After several months, she was just beginning to feel her worth again and was enjoying her own small apartment when one male customer decided she'd be better in bed than waiting tables. When she retreated from his advances, he became ornery and accused her of stealing from him. Her employers knew better than to believe him and sided with Mollie. But the incidents continued with other men, and Mollie became more and more afraid. She began to fear that she'd find someone hiding in her apartment or someone would follow her as she walked home from work at night. She never understood why she was so afraid, but she guessed it had something to do with the life she couldn't remember.

Finally, because she was so fearful and customers complained that she was rude or thoughtless, her employers asked her to leave. She knew that they'd tried longer than they should have to keep her on the job, but she just couldn't face those customers anymore. Her final check for four hundred dollars was more than she had coming, but they said it was to help her out until she found another job. But finding another job had proved difficult.

Just when her money was running out and the rent was due, Duke showed up at her door and told her to pack her bags. They were headed for San Francisco. Had he decided to quit his job and leave because of her? She had asked him, but he would never give her a straight answer.

As Mollie lay stretched out across the flowered bedspread, she wondered again why Duke, who could always find work and could hold a job, always managed to head her in another direction just when she needed a new direction.

They had both liked San Francisco, and Duke found a delivery job immediately. It took Mollie longer to find work, and once again it was Duke who found something for her and introduced her to the Andersons. John Anderson was a big, kindly man, and his pretty wife, Sally, had taken a chance hiring Mollie to work in their little seafood restaurant on the wharf. They even provided a nice studio apartment for her above the restaurant, and her lonely existence lasted there for twenty years. The Andersons were good to her and never let her get into a position where she could be embarrassed by a customer. They were the ones who also enrolled her and Duke in a signing class so she could finally talk to people and make other people understand her. Still, she didn't make friends easily, and Duke remained the only real friend she had. When the Andersons decided to sell the restaurant after twenty years and retire, Mollie was devastated. The young couple who became her new employers wanted young, efficient help, not an aging woman who was developing arthritis in every joint and could only talk with her hands.

Once again, she struggled to find employers who would be understanding, but business people wanted someone who could enhance their business, not be a detriment. And along with her job, Mollie had also lost the apartment above the restaurant.

With no funds and no place to live, Duke had insisted she move into his tiny, one-bedroom apartment with him. But Mollie had refused. He had already done too much for her, and she wasn't going to ask for more. She joined other homeless women on the streets, eating any available food and sleeping wherever she could—in an unlocked car, on a park bench, or curled up over a heat vent in the street, or in an alley. In those days, Mollie no longer cared about what happened to her. She prayed to die, even if it meant dying without knowing her real name. She just wanted to close her eyes and never wake up again, and every time she woke up, she was disappointed that God had let her down. She didn't even know why she prayed to God or why she was disappointed in him. She hadn't been inside a church in the last forty years and didn't know if she'd been in one before that. Somehow though, she knew that he was with her, she just didn't know why he bothered.

Mollie dozed under the lilac comforter, remembering once again that Duke, after an unusually rainy season when Mollie could never get dry or warm, had found her on the streets and told her to gather up her belongings because they were heading north. Mollie knew though that this time, Duke hated to leave. He had a good job, and Mollie suspected that he had a lady friend. She tried to dissuade him, but he refused to listen. They hitched a ride on the back of a farm implement truck and rode north to Sacramento. From there they hid out in a Southern Pacific freight car that took them through northern California and across Oregon to Portland. Mollie had yearned to see the Pacific Northwest just once in her life, and now she felt as though she'd finally arrived. Duke settled in as a janitor for the Salvation Army, and Mollie went job hunting. Duke had pleaded with her to get help from the Salvation Army, but, as always, she refused. No preachers or missions for her. When she couldn't find a job and her discontentment grew, she wanted to go farther north, maybe to Seattle.

Once more, knowing she'd go alone if she had to, Duke gave in to her wishes and managed to talk a fisherman into giving them a ride up the coast. While the old scow was docked in Grayport, they had decided to stay there. The sun had been shining, and Mollie was warm for the first time in months. It was late July, and Grayport looked good to them both. Duke had even vowed that he was through traveling, and Mollie knew he meant it. She would never ask him to leave Grayport. If she had to leave, she'd go alone. She had already asked too much of the wonderful, shabby man who had befriended her in Joplin. He had given her much, and she had given him nothing.

At first Mollie wasn't alarmed at the commotion outside her door. People were always moving about in the hall, discussing one thing or another in loud voices. No one ever bothered with her room, and even the maids, thinking the room was unoccupied, never checked the door.

This time, however, someone fumbled with a key in the broken lock, and Mollie heard a man's voice swearing loudly as he shoved on the door. She pulled the comforter up around her head, waiting for the inevitable. When next she stuck her head out, a chubby, middle-aged man with a goatee stood over her, glaring down at her.

Mollie, naked under the ghastly lilac comforter, stared back.

11

The phone next to him on the prescription counter rang sharply, jarring Gil out of his concentration, trying to read a doctor's difficult handwriting. When he picked up the phone, he was surprised to hear the police chief's voice on the other end.

"You said you wanted to know if there was any new information on Mollie," the chief said.

Gil was instantly alert. "You bet. Has she been found? Is she all right?"

The chief laughed. "None of the above, but it seems you didn't have to worry about Mollie freezing to death. The old girl really knows how to take care of herself. She's been holed up in a room at the Edgemoor Hotel."

"The Edgemoor? How would she ever be able to manage that?" Gil knew that hotels had ways of keeping people like Mollie out of their hotel rooms.

"We don't know for sure, but it looks like she's been there for at least two weeks."

"Two weeks?" Gil was astonished that Mollie could pull off such a feat. "Did someone provide her with a room or what?"

"Evidently she provided herself with a room, one that is seldom used on the utility floor. The manager told me that several staff members have been in trouble because food has been missing from the kitchen, and hotel patron's clothes have been missing from the laundry. After discovering that Mollie was in the room near both the kitchen and laundry room, the mystery has been solved, and his employees have been exonerated."

"How did they discover that she was there?" Gil was still stupefied by Mollie's audacity.

"Evidently the assistant manager, who knew the lock was broken on the outside of the room, uses it occasionally for his own purposes. He would tell his 'person of interest' just to go there and wait inside the room until he showed up for their fun and games. Since he was the one who was supposed to make sure all the locks were working properly throughout the hotel, no one ever questioned the lock on the door on the bottom floor. The room was seldom used, mostly saved in case of overbookings, whatever."

"And when his girlfriend couldn't get into the room, she blew the whistle," Gil said.

"Exactly. She discreetly found the assistant manager and told him the door was locked. He went downstairs to check for himself, and finding the door locked, he became angry and put a shoulder to it. Imagine his surprise when he found Mollie in bed, naked as a jaybird?"

"Poor Mollie! She must have been terrified. Was she arrested?"

"No," the chief chuckled. "She escaped somehow. While the assistant manager and the girlfriend were trying to figure out how to save his butt, Mollie must have dressed and slipped out somehow. The manager suspects that his assistant manager let Mollie go to protect his own skin, but the guy swears he didn't. At any rate, the hotel will soon have a new assistant manager, and Mollie is out of a plush hiding place."

"Will she be arrested when she's found?"

"I doubt it. The Edgemoor people know she won't be back, and no one has charged her with anything. I did ask my officers to keep a lookout for her just for her own safety's sake. That's another reason I thought you might like to know what's happened."

"Thanks, Chief. I'm almost finished with my day here, so I'll swing by the Grand on my way home. After her life of luxury, she'll be miserable in that cold, smelly place." Gil hung up and breathed a deep sigh of relief. He was glad Mollie was still in Grayport and that, up until last night, she'd been safe and warm.

Gil had promised Pam, who was working late at the school, that he'd pick her up. Boyd had borrowed her van again to go car shopping. If Gil was going to check on Mollie, he'd better let Pam know. He dialed the school and left a message for Pam to call him back when she was near a phone. Then he tried to focus once more on the chicken-scratched prescription.

When Pam called back, she sounded worried. "It's nothing serious, Pam. I just wanted to tell you that I have an errand to run before I pick you up. I may be a little late."

"What kind of errand?" she sounded irritated with him, so he hesitated before answering her. He never knew how she'd react to mention of Mollie. "Is it Mollie?" she asked before he could answer.

"She's been found, Pam. She had moved into a room at the Edgemoor, and she was discovered last night."

"The Edgemoor?" Pam exclaimed then chuckled. "You have to give her a lot of credit for being a pretty smart old broad. Was she arrested?"

"No, she's disappeared again. She might be back at the Grand. I told Chief Burgess that I'd check before I went home."

"Gil, it's too cold for her in that place. We have some extra blankets at home. Why don't you pick me up first and we can go by the house and get them? I'll go to the hotel with you."

Gil was surprised but pleased. He could hardly answer for the lump in his throat. "That'll be great, Pam. See you in a while."

With Jeanne's help reading the difficult prescription, Gil finally succeeded in finishing it, and between the two of them, the rest of the stack went swiftly. All waiting customers had received their medicine and left. Jeanne went about her other business. Gil pulled the paper with Keith Weldon's phone numbers out of his pocket.

Because of the two-hour time difference, the *St. Louis Post-Dispatch* would be closed by now, and Gil debated whether to try to reach the guy at home. Finally, his mind made up, he dialed the home phone number that was written on the little piece of paper.

A man answered on the second ring, and Gil realized that it was Keith Weldon he was speaking with. Without any more hesitation, Gil explained his concern for Mollie and told the other man what he knew of Mollie's background.

"Sure sounds like you might be onto something," Weldon told him. "Especially if the old lady has had amnesia for all these years."

"There may be nothing to any of this, but I thought it was worth a phone call to see what you thought," Gil told him.

"No problem, Gil. I'll snoop around, ask some questions, and get back to you. Tell Harv hello for me."

"Will do. Thanks, Keith, for your help."

As Gill left the pharmacy, heading for his car, he glanced toward Ostergood's Flower Shop. The bitter cold wind whipped through his overcoat and bit at his ears and nose. Before he gave a second thought to what he was doing, he retreated back across the street and entered the flower shop. Mr. Ostergood greeted him warmly.

"Come to give me your Christmas order, Gil?" the older man asked.

"My Christmas order?" Gil was nonplussed by the question, and then he remembered his annual poinsettia order for his clerks. Every year since he'd opened the drugstore, he'd given each of his employees a bright red poinsettia with a bonus plus a couple for Pam who used them for her decorations. Gil had totally forgotten. "Yes, I'd better do that, but I forgot my list. It would be the same as last year's, if you still have it."

Mr. Ostergood promptly found Gil's list in his orderly files. "I'll deliver the flowers to your store on Christmas Eve as usual," the old man promised.

"While I'm here, Mr. Ostergood, could you put me together a bouquet of pink carnations, the silk kind?"

Mr. Ostergood eyed him warily but said, "I have some already made up if you'd like to see them." He pointed to a shelf toward the rear of the store, out of the way of all the Christmas displays. "But if you could use something that isn't pink, this one might do." He picked up a basket of bright red silk carnations with springs of tiny white flowers and greenery stuck in among the flowers. A red bow and streamers of red-and-white Christmas ribbons spilled over the side of the basket, and a "Merry Christmas" poke stuck up in the middle.

Gil had thought that he wanted pink carnations, but the Christmas basket was beautiful and would brighten any cold, dreary place. "I'll take it," Gil said finally. He couldn't help noticing the disapproval on Mr. Ostergood's face as he wrapped green floral paper around Gil's purchase.

With the bright bouquet on the seat beside him, he drove to McCausland Elementary, and Pam, who had been watching for him, hopped into the passenger side. She spotted the flowers immediately. "I don't think those are for me," she said, but Gil noticed that she was smiling.

"I thought they might cheer Mollie up."

"Too cold for real ones, huh?"

He glanced at her, surprised. "How did you know about those?"

"Mr. Ostergood, bless his heart, thought you were up to something, and he thought I should know. Really, Gil, you shouldn't act so suspicious when you're around that old busybody."

"I thought you'd be upset it you knew. After all, you hadn't liked sharing me with Mollie."

Pam laughed, a sound that swelled Gil's heart. One thing he loved about her was her usually sunny disposition and her light, sweet laughter. Of late, Pam's sense of humor had been displaced with stress and, particularly, with irritation for him. "At first I resented the dirty old woman. She had your undivided attention, and I felt short-changed. I needed you and your attention on *my* needs. I was being a spoiled brat, Gil. I understand now why you feel the way you do, and I admire you for caring so much."

"Can you imagine caring for someone who eats out of garbage cans and wears clothes she's stolen from a hotel's laundry room?"

Pam laughed. "Did she actually steal clothes from the Edgemoor?"

"Yes, and she ate from their kitchen, and she slept in one of their warm, snuggly beds."

"Good for her," Pam chuckled. "That old girl has spunk."

After a short stop at their house so Pam could collect blankets, they arrived at the Grand Hotel. Pam pulled the blankets from the back seat and headed for the door. "I guess we won't ever want these back," she told Gil. "Imagine the critters that must live in Mollie's hair."

"How can you think that? After all, she bathed at the Edgemoor."

The decaying building, with the cold wind blowing through, wouldn't offer Mollie much protection from the plummeting temperatures. Gil shivered as he and Pam climbed the stairs as quietly as possible and listened at Mollie's door. There were no sounds from inside the room, so Gil pushed the door open and stepped inside. To his disappointment, Mollie wasn't there.

"I thought she'd be back here by now," he said. "Maybe she has another warm spot she frequents."

"She's no dummy, Gil. She'll get in out of the cold."

Pam unzipped the Boy Scout sleeping bag that Boyd had long outgrown and threw it on Mollie's cot. She piled the other blankets nearby on the floor. "Guess if she doesn't use these, someone else will."

Gil pulled back the heavy canvas on the window and saw Mollie on the rocky beach below. "She'll use them, and before very long," he told Pam, "we'd better get out of here." He dumped the frozen black flowers out of the vase and into a battered cardboard box he'd found on the floor and replaced the vase with the Christmas basket. Then they hurriedly left.

As they drove out of the hotel's circular driveway, Mollie was just coming around the building to the hotel's front door. She had her head down and moved slowly as if she was racked with pain. She never saw the white car driving away.

"Feel like shopping?" Gil asked, knowing neither of them had finished purchasing their Christmas gifts.

"Only if you buy me dinner first."

"What about the kids?"

"They've got all sorts of plans tonight, and no one will be home until ten o'clock. We've got the evening to ourselves."

Gil raised his eyebrows. "Are you sure you just don't want to go straight home?" he asked, hinting.

"Gil, how can you think such things when you just took your other girlfriend flowers and I got nothing?"

"But I was suggesting that I'd give you something," he said, cocking his head mischievously.

"Just drive, you idiot. I'm starving, and we need to shop. The rest can wait until later."

"But the kids will be home by ten o'clock. Don't toy with me, Pam. Remember, I know where to find the other woman."

12

As they drove away from the old Grand, Gil and Pam had no idea of the fear and desolation that had gripped Mollie as she fled from the Edgemoor Hotel. After her days in the warm room, the contrasting bitter cold was harder for Mollie to bear. Her aching feet and legs had hardly carried her away from the Edgemoor, and her heart still pounded with the fear of being arrested by the Grayport police.

She had managed to make it down the hill and into the alley behind Petersen's hardware store. She had tried the alley entrance to the store and found it unlocked. It looked to Mollie like a previous visitor had broken the lock. She had slipped into the basement and warmed herself next to the antiquated furnace. Only empty crates and boxes occupied the rest of the space in the unlocked part of the basement. A large silver padlock on an opposite heavy door prevented anyone from entering the rest of the basement where Mollie assumed the valuable stuff was kept.

Mollie had known that she couldn't stay long in the basement. She wasn't sure if the furnace would be checked when the store opened in the morning, and she couldn't risk being found. She just needed to rest before finishing her trek to the old Grand. Her chest ached, and her stomach was upset. She'd left the decanter of wine behind when she'd made her hasty departure from the Edgemoor, and she'd longed for a sip of the brew to warm her insides. She'd dozed fitfully on her bed of empty lawn mower crates. She'd always been able to sleep anywhere, so it was good to know that her stay at the Edgemoor hadn't spoiled that.

During the dark, early hours of morning, she'd heard young male voices in the alley. She'd held her breath, afraid of being discovered. *Lord, don't let me cough,* she'd prayed. What if this part of the basement was the hangout for every pothead in town? They wouldn't care what happened to her. Maybe the boy that hit her would be one of them. She didn't want to meet up with him again.

Finally, the voices faded away, and Mollie was able to doze again. This time her fatigue overcame her, and she slept soundly. When she awoke, she was surprised to hear boards creaking overhead as people walked about the hardware store. She had no idea what time it was, but she knew she'd been in the basement too long. She stood up and tried to shake the stiffness out of her joints, something that was becoming more impossible with each passing day.

With the pea jacket pulled tightly around her and a long, knitted scarf around her head, covering most of her face, she'd left the basement. It was daylight now, and the alley was deserted as she'd shuffled along, staying close to the buildings to avoid the cold wind that whistled around her. At the First Interstate Bank's time and temperature corner, Mollie had discovered, to her surprise, that it was late afternoon, and the temperature had warmed up to twenty-eight degrees. No one on the streets seemed to notice her, and the one officer she saw in a police cruiser showed no interest in her at all. Behind the liquor store, she'd looked in the dumpster for a bourbon bottle that still had liquor in it, but no one threw away good bourbon. Even the ones with bad seals or other damage never turned up in the dumpsters, much to Mollie's chagrin. Behind the Pick'N Pack, Mollie had rummaged through the dumpster and came up with two packages of frozen oatmeal cookies with a few cookies missing out of each package.

As Mollie emerged from the alley behind the supermarket, to begin the block-long walk across the vacant lot to the Grand, she heard hoots and jeers from people in a car somewhere behind her. She paid little attention. All she wanted now was to get back to her room at the hotel even if it lacked the comforts of the Edgemoor. She stumbled across the rocks, the wind off the river whipping through her clothes, chilling her to the bone. By the time she'd reached the steps to the hotel's second floor, she was exhausted. It took every last ounce of strength to climb the stairs and make it to the abandoned room she called home.

As she pushed open the door, the vivid red carnations were the first sight to greet her eyes. A low cry of surprise escaped her lips. She leaned over the table and fondled the red silk petals. She didn't have to guess who'd brought them. Her heart swelled with joy, and tears spilled down her rough, chapped cheeks. A Christmas bouquet! She hadn't celebrated Christmas since she'd been on the streets. While she'd worked for the Andersons, they'd always given her a small gift at Christmastime, and she'd bought them a box of candy each year, but no one had given her anything since. Not even Duke. She didn't even know what he did at Christmas. For the first time, she began to appreciate that someone besides Duke really cared about her, and for the first time since the man in the white car had started following her around, she was glad. She knew he meant her no harm.

As she sat down on the cot to pull off the green boots, she noticed the sleeping bag opened invitingly on her cot and the pile of blankets nearby. She rubbed the fabric of the sleeping bag and smiled, deeming it quite luxurious. Not as luxurious as the Edgemoor but luxurious anyhow. Then she lay down on the cot, and without zipping the bag shut, she pulled it up snugly under her chin and drifted off into an exhausted sleep.

Mollie slept fitfully, plagued with dreams that frightened her. Once more, she was at the Edgemoor being chased by the police. She heard cackles and low chants as voices taunted her, and three faces stared down at her. Once again, she was back forty years, and three men were holding her down, hurting her. She tried to scream and woke up to realize that she wasn't dreaming. Someone was laying on top of her, his weight suffocating her. A second person was throwing her dishes on the floor, shattering anything that wasn't plastic, laughing menacingly as he did it.

With strength Mollie didn't know she had, she reared up suddenly, causing her attacker to fall to the floor. As she tried to free herself from the sleeping bag, he grabbed her and nearly pulled her head off as he dragged her to the floor. Finally, out of the bag, she escaped to the corner near the bed and cowered there while both men kicked her with heavy boots. She longed to pass out. Instead she vomited.

"Jeez! She got me," one of them said. "It smells. Let's get outta here."

Mollie heard them leave, heard a car engine start up and roar away from the hotel. She stayed in the corner, sobbing. The pain in her chest was unbearable, and blood dripped from a wound to her head. She found a rag—maybe it was one of her confiscated shirts—and wiped the blood from her eyes. She knew that she had to get help. If she didn't, she might die, and dying without knowing who she was still frightened her. Surely God knew who she was, but she needed to know for herself. She'd always hoped her demise would be peaceful and that Duke would bury her someplace where it was pretty. This hotel wasn't pretty, and she had no intention of being a murder victim. Somehow that idea wasn't new to her. Why did she feel like history was repeating itself? During the attack, she'd thought she was dreaming, a dream from her past. Had something like this happened to her before?

Mollie summoned up enough strength to search the dark corner with her hand, hoping to find the paper sack she'd thrown there, the one with the drugstore man's phone numbers on it. She found the wadded-up bag on the floor behind her and carefully straightened it out. It was too dark to see the bold handwriting that Mollie knew was on it. She shoved the paper into her pocket and then forced herself to crawl to the sink where she was able to hoist herself into an upright position. Dizziness overcame her, but she fought against unconsciousness. She was finally able to make it to her cot and located her boots which were nearly impossible for her to pull on. She knew she needed them, or her feet would freeze. It wasn't going to be easy, but Mollie had to get to a telephone.

*****

Gil didn't know why there was a phone on his side of the queen-size bed, except maybe the telephone hookup was on that wall. At any rate, when the phone jangled close to his head, nearly scaring him out of his wits, he remembered again why he wished the phone was on Pam's side. As he struggled to find the receiver, he tried to get his eyes open enough to read the red numbers on the digital clock. "Midnight?" he squawked when he was finally able to see. "Who'd be calling us at midnight?" He knew both Hayworth sons and Traci were home and in bed. Pam was stirring next to him, so his family was all accounted for. He picked up the receiver and heard strange guttural sounds.

"Damned idiots!" He slammed the phone back onto its cradle.

Pam moaned and rolled over. Gil pulled the blankets back up around his ears, trying to go back to sleep. Then he heard a soft knock on the bedroom door.

"Dad?" It was Tim.

"What now?" Gil barked at his son and sat up in bed.

Tim's shadowy figure stepped into the bedroom. "Dad, I answered the phone about the same time you did. I don't think it was a prank call."

"Then who do you think it was?"

"I think someone was crying. I wondered if it was Mollie and if maybe she's hurt."

"Where on earth would she be calling from?"

"I don't know, Dad. I just wondered if we should call the police and alert them."

Gil sat up on the side of the bed. "No, I think maybe we should just take a look for ourselves first. The police would just scare her to death if they go poking around."

"I'll get dressed," Tim said and headed back down the hall.

Gil tugged on his blue jeans and pulled an old faded Sonics sweatshirt over his head.

"You're not going without me," Pam told him as she climbed out of bed and pulled on her old sweatpants and shirt. "She may need a woman's help." Gil wasn't going to argue with her. Later, if they found Mollie safe and sound, both he and Pam might want to throttle Tim for disturbing their sleep, but for now he appreciated her company.

When all three were snug in their warm coats and each carried a working flashlight, Pam wrote a quick note to Boyd and Traci, in case they woke up and found them gone, and then they left the house.

A full moon floated high in the cloudless sky, lighting their way to Tim's old blue Chevy, the easiest car to get out of the driveway at this hour.

There was very little activity on Grayport streets, and Tim drove slowly through town, up and down streets and through alleys. Finally, they decided to check the hotel. All three turned their flashlights on as they entered the dark, creepy building and climbed the stairs.

"Gil! Is that blood?" Pam was aiming her light at the dark spot on a step.

Gil tested the spot with his finger and discovered fresh blood "Oh my god!" He didn't wait for the others. He bounded up the stairs with Pam and Tim close behind. Mollie's door stood open, and the flashlight revealed a room in shambles. Gil's flowers were strewn all over the floor, trampled by someone's feet. The sleeping bag on the floor next to the cot was covered with blood.

"She can't be far away," Tim said. "Not bleeding that badly!" He started for the door with Pam and Gil following.

"The closest phone would be at the all-night service station two blocks away," Gil said. "Could she make it that far?"

Tim's tires squealed as they left the hotel's rutted driveway, but Tim had already decided that should a policeman show up, that policeman would come in handy about now.

At the service station, a startled attendant eyed them as they jumped out of the car and ran toward him. "Where's your phone?" Gil shouted. The attendant pointed toward the station's lube bay, and they found the phone just inside the door. They also found what they were looking for. There was blood all over the phone's receiver.

"Did you see an old lady around here earlier? She used this phone," Tim told the attendant.

"You mean old Mollie? Sure, I saw her." He paused. "Well, I didn't actually see her. I was working on a car and noticed her over there by the phone. I didn't pay much attention to her. She can't talk, you know."

"Yeah, we know," Gil said, "but we think she's around here someplace."

"She may be in the restroom. My boss lets her use it to wash up sometimes." He pointed to the rear of the building. "It's around back."

Tim was the first to arrive at the door and tried the knob. "It's locked." Pam ran back around the building to ask for the key.

"We never lock it, mainly because of Mollie," the attendant explained. "Maybe she locked it from inside."

Pam ran back to tell Gil and Tim the bad news. Both men put their shoulders to the door and shoved. The door gave a little, but not enough to gain entrance. "I don't think the door's locked," Gil said. "I think maybe she's fallen against it." He looked at his wife. "Pam, I think it's time to call the police. We're going to need their help and probably an ambulance."

Pam ran, once again, to the front of the building to call the police while Gil and Tim continued to shove on the door. Within minutes, a police car, with two officers inside, pulled into the service station. Gil explained the situation to them, and they examined the door.

"We're wasting time standing here," the tall, lanky officer said when he heard that Mollie might be badly injured. "Let's get this door off."

While the older officer went to his car for a crowbar, the other three applied their weight to the door and were surprised when they heard moans from inside. Then quite unexpectedly, the pressure against the inside of the door eased.

"She must've moved," Tim exclaimed.

The door opened wide enough for Gil to slip inside. Mollie was sprawled on the floor of the tiny room, her face and clothing covered in blood. Gil carefully moved her feet away from the door and opened it for the officers. He heard Pam gasp.

"Better call for an ambulance," the older office said.

"It's on the way," Pam told him, and distant wails of a siren could be heard coming across town. When the ambulance arrived and the attendants had secured Mollie inside, they all watched in shock and silence as a battered Mollie was whisked away accompanied by the blaring siren.

"Do we need to go to the hospital so she'll know she has friends with her?" Tim asked.

"I doubt if she'd even know we were there," Pam said with sadness. "At least she'll have a warm bed to sleep in again tonight."

"I know the ambulance driver," Gil continued. "He said someone would contact us if we're needed. Perhaps we should get some rest ourselves. Who knows what tomorrow will bring."

Pam pulled both Gil and Tim close. "Who would have done such a horrible thing to Mollie? They nearly killed her."

Gil nodded, unable to speak. Pam had just voiced his worse fear, and Mollie could still die before the night was over. And if what her friend Duke said was true, Mollie would hate dying without knowing who she really was. It broke his heart.

The police officer questioned the station attendant. "Did you see anyone on the street tonight who might have done this to Mollie?"

"Naw, like I told Mr. Hayworth, I was workin' on a car that I had to get finished, and I wasn't really payin' attention to much else. There had been some kids squealin' up and down the street in a fancy van, and I got nervous, bein' here alone and all, but they didn't come in here."

"Which way were they headed, do you know?"

"That way." He pointed toward the old hotel. "They may have turned into the hotel's driveway, but, like I say, I just don't know."

"You say it was a fancy van. What did it look like?" the officer asked.

"It was big, like a van, and it could have been black." He thought for a minute. "Yes, I'm pretty sure it was black. It turned around under the corner light."

Gil felt Tim stiffen beside him. Bailey Nickerson had a black van.

"Did you notice any Star Wars pictures on the side?" Tim asked.

"Can't say for sure if it was Star Wars, but there was something painted on the side."

Tim's shoulders drooped, and the officer eyed him.

"Do you know who it was?" he asked.

"Not for sure," Tim told him, "but Bailey Nickerson has a van like that. He would also enjoy tormenting Mollie."

"We'll check him out. Mollie didn't deserve the treatment she got tonight. She never bothers anyone." The older officer seemed as upset by the night's events as they all were. "We'll keep you posted, Mr. Hayworth. Glad you cared enough to get involved."

As they drove home, Tim was quiet.

"Do you really think Bailey is capable of something as ugly as beating up an old woman?" Gil asked him.

"A month ago, I wouldn't have thought so, but I see Bailey differently now, Dad. I think he's capable, and I think he did it."

Gil's heart ached for his son as well as for Mollie. Tim had idolized Bailey Nickerson, refusing to believe anything bad about him. It had to be hard to see your idol fall so far. Gil thanked God for showing Tim the truth before he'd been caught up in the same ugliness.

"We'd better get some sleep," he told Pam and Tim as they pulled into their driveway. "Tomorrow's going to be a long day."

13

Gil spent a restless night knowing there was nothing he could do at the hospital but anxious to be there anyhow. Pam had been restless, too, but she'd fallen soundly asleep toward morning, and Gil didn't want to awaken her. He slipped quietly out of bed, slipped into his robe and slippers, and padded downstairs to what Pam liked to refer to as "the study." Granted there were two walls of shelves lined with books, but there was also a computer and all its paraphernalia, plus a television set with video games strewn all around.

The room was anything but Pam's original idea for a study. Gil opened the drapes to let in the dim Saturday morning light and then settled himself into his overstuffed chair to search for peace for himself and for Mollie. He prayed that she wouldn't die. He prayed that somehow he'd be given a chance to find out who she was and where she came from. He prayed that her attacker or attackers would be found swiftly.

By the time the rest of the family began to move around, Gil's restlessness had eased. He sat down with Pam at the kitchen table and accepted the offered cup of coffee.

"How soon are you going to the hospital?" Pam asked him.

"Pretty soon. I want to see if Mollie has regained consciousness or if there's any news of her condition before I go to the store."

"I would like to go and stay with her for a while. She may be frightened when she wakes up in the hospital."

Gil reached over and took Pam's hand in his. She was so special. Christmas was fast approaching. There was shopping to be finished, the house needed decorating, and baking needed to be done, plus she had all the busyness at school, and still Pam was willing to sit at the hospital with Mollie.

"I love you, Pam," he told her. "I guess you know that."

She grinned sleepily. "I know that, and I love you even though I sometimes wonder what goes on in that head of yours."

"Admit it. You're curious about Mollie too."

"I admit it. At first I thought you were out of your mind for making such a big deal of her, but now I'm wondering how she ended up being a bag lady, and not an ordinary one at that." She laughed. "Not too many bag people would dare to infiltrate the rooms at a swanky hotel."

"I think what bothers me is that she's been wandering around all these years without knowing who she is. Duke was no help to her, obviously, in finding out where she came from. He just accepted her for who she was and let her tag along with him."

Pam patted his hand. "I know you'll get answers. I really hope you do." She busied herself scrambling eggs and pouring juice for the rest of the family. "Mollie must have been terrified last night, Gil. But imagine how much spunk it took for her to get out of that hotel and get to a phone to call for help. I just hope that spunk gets her through the next few days."

"I hope so too." Gil stood up and started setting the table then carried the juice to the table. "Besides the hospital, what are your plans for today?"

"Traci has pageant rehearsal at the church this afternoon, Boyd has basketball practice later today, and Tim seems to be 'hanging loose,' as he says. Oh, and don't forget Traci has a date for the school dance tonight. Everything's under control," she joked.

Gil shook his head in amazement. Pam remembered every-thing, and he had such a one-track mind he'd even forgotten about the biggest event in Traci's life—the Christmas dance. He couldn't even remember her date's name. Fathers were supposed to know that stuff, weren't they? It was some kind of "Father's Code." He glanced at his two sons and daughter who had joined him at the table. They were doing okay. Perhaps he hadn't been such a bad father, just an absent-minded one.

"So tonight's the big dance, huh, Trace? You're going with Sammy?"

"Sammy who, Dad? I don't think I even know a Sammy. I'm going with Scott Peterson." She grinned at his embarrassment. "That's okay, Dad. At least you remembered there was a dance."

"So what's with Mollie?" Boyd asked as he devoured his scrambled eggs. "I heard you guys leave last night and came down to see what was going on. That's when I found your note."

"Someone beat her up last night," Tim said. "They did a really good job on her too. She's in the hospital." He explained to Boyd and Traci how they'd found her at the service station and how she'd been transported to the hospital. "I won't be surprised to learn that Bailey Nickerson and his friends are the ones who did it."

"Your old buddy?" Boyd was surprised. "I thought you liked that guy."

"I did," Tim told him, "until I saw his mean streak that day he was bothering Mollie in the alley. I realized then how wrong I'd been about the guy."

"And we're all glad of that," Gil put in. "Your mother and I are going to the hospital this morning early. We'd appreciate it if you'd drag down the Christmas decorations from the attic, and also it would be a big help if you could pick out a tree from one of the lots. Maybe tonight we can get the tree up and decorated so it will begin to look like Christmas around here."

"Sure, Dad, we can handle that," Tim said. "Except Miss Priss here might not want to get dirty because of her big date tonight."

Traci's face turned pink, but this time she knew Tim was teasing her, so she took it in stride. She also was glad Tim was his old self and not the mean-mouthed Tim he'd been in the not-too-distant past.

Gil and Pam left the kitchen mess for the kids to clean up and drove to the hospital in separate cars. The temperature had climbed above freezing, and the streets were dry. Gil was glad. He always dreaded the steep incline to the hospital if the roads were slippery. Why cities built their hospitals on the highest hills was beyond Gil's imagination. Maybe they wanted to provide their patients rooms with a view, but it only made for anxious ambulance drivers during winter weather.

Grayport General was built on the same row of hills as the Edgemoor Hotel but farther away from downtown Grayport. Patients on one side of the building could see fancy hillside homes from their windows while patients on the opposite side of the corridor could look out over the harbor. Gil thought that would be the most desirable view, but his one hospital trip two years back, to remove his appendix, had given him a room with a view, but he hadn't much cared.

On the second floor of the brightly lit hospital, Gil and Pam found Mollie's room and entered quietly. Without all the layers of clothing, Mollie looked small and frail in the hospital bed. Her wounds had been cleaned, and her matted gray hair had been combed and straightened. Gil thought that she looked slightly better than when they'd last seen her. They were both concerned about her shallow, raspy breathing.

Gil leaned over the bed and took a small hand in his own. "Mollie," he whispered, "can you hear me?" Her eyelids fluttered, but she didn't open them.

A nurse came into the room. "Are you relatives?" she asked curtly.

"No, just friends," Gil told her.

"The ambulance driver didn't have any information about this woman. We're authorized by the police department to take care of her, but our admissions person needs to talk to someone. We don't usually take indigent patients."

"My wife or I will speak to admissions. Thanks for your concern." Gil understood that the nurse's curtness was not necessarily directed at them. The hospital had rules, and those rules were being broken. Gil experienced the same thing at the pharmacy when dealing with bureaucrats.

"What's Mollie's condition?" Pam asked from the opposite side of the bed.

"The test results aren't all back yet, so the doctor will have to get in touch with you when they are."

"Thanks," Gil said to the white uniformed back that disappeared through the door and into the hall.

"Who *is* going to pay for this, Gil?" Pam asked, worried. "We can't afford any horrendous hospital bills."

"I know, but we'll work something out with admissions. We can't have them putting Mollie back out on the street."

"Of course not," Pam said softly, but Gil knew she was mentally figuring costs in her head. "I'd better go down and straighten things out with admissions and let the hospital know who to contact when they get test results."

After Pam left, Gil stood by Mollie's bedside, willing her to open her eyes, but the small figure remained motionless. As he held her thin, bony fingers in his hand, his heart ached. Who was she? Where was she from? After all those years, would it be possible to find her family? Gil hoped so. With all his heart, he hoped so.

*****

Gil had opened the store on time and was involved in sorting out overnight phone messages who needed prescription refills or who needed to see him later for pharmacy needs when the telephone rang. When he picked up the receiver, he expected to hear Pam's voice. She had said she'd call from the hospital if there was any news. Instead, it was Keith Weldon.

"You sure get to work late," the Midwesterner laughed. "It's almost time for lunch back here. Just wanted to let you know that I have some information for you, something I stumbled onto right here at the *Post-Dispatch*."

Gil's pulse raced. "What have you found?"

"One of the old guys here told me there used to be a reporter here years ago who was investigating a crime that nearly drove him nuts. He was looking for a missing woman, one that he never found and get this. It happened forty-three years ago. I decided that was pretty darned close to your time frame."

"Where's the reporter now?"

"He's retired, and he and his wife live at the Lake of the Ozarks. I've got his phone number if you want to try to link your woman to his."

"Do I?" Gil was excited. "I know it's a long shot, but it's certainly worth a try."

Gil jotted down the reporter's name and number, thanked Keith Weldon for his trouble, and hung up. He stood holding the piece of paper for several minutes, thinking. He knew the missing woman was probably not Mollie. It would be too much of a coincidence to find out that Mollie was the woman the reporter had been trying to trace for all those years. And what if she was? Maybe finding out who she was would put her in some kind of danger. Or what if she had family that would not like to hear that she'd become a bag lady. Still Gil knew he'd have to call that number on that slip of paper.

He waited until Jeanne came in to work just before noon and explained to her that he was going home for lunch, something he seldom did, especially on a Saturday. He usually brought a sandwich from home or had one of the clerks get him something from the Sub Shop. Today, he had to make an important phone call, and he knew Pam would want to hear about it too. He called the hospital and asked for Mollie's room. Pam answered on the first ring. He explained why he was going home for lunch, and she agreed to meet him there.

When he bounded up the steps and into the back door of his house, Tim was coming out with an armload of boxes for the trash.

"Whoa, Dad," Tim exclaimed. "You must want lunch in a hurry."

"Actually, it's not lunch I'm interested in," Gil told him. "I want to call someone in Missouri who might know who Mollie is." He explained to his son about the call from Keith Weldon.

"Way to go, Dad. Let's hope you're on the right track."

Pam was home, but Gil didn't stop to eat the sandwich she had prepared. He went straight to the telephone. His hand was shaking as he dialed the number on the paper. A woman with a strident voice and a heavy Midwestern twang answered the phone.

"Mrs. Patterson?" Gil asked. "Is your husband home?"

"Ed? Sure, he is, but he's down by the lake. Can he call you back?"

Gil had to hold the receiver away from his ear so the woman's loud voice wouldn't deafen him. "I'm calling from Washington State, Mrs. Patterson. I need to speak to him about a missing woman."

"Oh my goodness!" she shrieked. "Not her again! Hold on a minute. I'll go outside and call him."

Gil could hear her screeching for her husband, then a door banged, and pots and pans clanked near the telephone. Gil waited. Just when he'd decided that Ed Patterson wasn't coming to the phone, he heard a man's slow drawl in the receiver.

"Mr. Patterson, my name is Gil Hayworth, and I'm calling from Grayport on the Washington coast. Someone at the *Post-Dispatch* told me that you had some information about a woman you were looking for forty-some years ago."

"Ain't much to tell," the man drawled. "I could never track her down. What's your interest?"

"We have a bag lady who recently showed up in Grayport that has amnesia. She has a male friend who says he boarded a freight train with her in Joplin, Missouri, some forty-plus years ago."

There was dead silence on the other end of the line. When Ed Patterson finally spoke, he sounded as if the wind had been knocked out of him. "You don't suppose it's her?" He spoke so low Gil could barely hear him.

When Ed Patterson regained his composure, he said, "I'll tell you all I can remember. You'd have to check the file at the *Post-Dispatch* to get the full story. We had three men terrorizing the whole State of Missouri, raping and murdering women," he told Gil. "In northeastern Missouri, they murdered an old gentleman just to rob him of a few dollars, and then they raped a teenage girl near Columbia and another just south of Sedalia. They also walked into a farmhouse and raped and murdered the mother of five children. Every law enforcement man in this State was looking for a black '49 Chevy with Oklahoma license plates. Their route seemed to be across Missouri from east to west, so their trackers expected them to eventually show up in Oklahoma. Sure enough! They were finally apprehended north of Claremore, Oklahoma. When I heard about the missing woman from Camdenton, Missouri, I was afraid for her.

If she'd somehow met up with those men, her life wouldn't be worth a dime."

"Was Camdenton on their route?" Gil asked.

"By my estimation it was, but if they stopped there, no one spotted them. I did some investigating there myself, but everyone seemed to think she'd just got fed up with her preacher husband and left with another man. At first, her husband and two young boys thought differently. She'd disappeared the evening before her youngest son's tenth birthday. Early that evening, she'd discovered she was out of birthday candles for his cake, so she walked to a small neighborhood market just a few blocks away. She never returned."

"Why did the townspeople think she'd left her husband?"

"They told me she was a young pretty girl with lots of spunk, and her husband was a Baptist preacher, somewhat of a strict preacher from what I understood and quite a few years older than she was. Friends closest to the family though said that they thought she was happy with her family and with her life, but there were some men in town who'd hoped she would leave her husband so they could show her a good time."

"Do you think she left of her own accord?"

"Nope, I don't," Ed Patterson said quietly into the phone. "Right about that time, I heard about a truck driver who'd found a woman on the road near Joplin. Seems he saw something that looked like a pile of clothing laying in a heap on the pavement in front of him. But when he stopped his big rig to investigate, he discovered it was more than clothing. It was a woman. Her clothes had been ripped to shreds, and she was covered with blood. Someone had tried, unsuccessfully, to cut her throat."

Gil swallowed hard, the words sinking in. Mollie couldn't speak. Duke had told him that he'd thought someone had tried to cut her throat.

"The truck driver radioed for an ambulance," the old reporter continued. "After he gave a police report, he took off in his truck, knowing the woman was safely in the hands of the authorities. When I learned about the woman, I headed to Joplin and found out she had been admitted to the hospital. Besides having her throat cut, she'd been raped repeatedly. She was listed as a Jane Doe because she carried no identification, and no one came looking for her."

"So you know what she looked like?"

"Nope. Before I got to the hospital and even before she was out of danger, she stole a dress that belonged to the woman in the room with her and slipped out of the hospital, unnoticed. No one has seen her since."

"Didn't the preacher wonder if the woman was his wife?"

"Nope. He changed his mind and decided to believe the rumors that were going around town. I think it was easier for him to believe that his wife was safe somewhere with another man than that she'd been raped and nearly murdered."

"How could he live with that? Not knowing for sure?"

"Who knows? But he refused to listen when I tried to convince him that his wife might be the injured woman."

"So you think she did run into those three men?"

"I think so, but we had no way of knowing for sure. I thought if I could find her, we'd learn the truth, but I could never find a trace of her anywhere."

"Do you remember her name?"

"Do I? It's embedded in my brain. It's Mary Margaret Norris. What's the woman there called?"

"We call her Mollie, but that was the name given to her by her traveling companion. He'd thought maybe she was a gangster's moll and had double-crossed someone. Her throat had been bandaged and bloody, he told me, so it could have been from a cut." Gil told Ed Patterson the story that Duke had related to him about the couple's train-hopping trip west.

"Sure would make my day if she turned out to be my missing woman. I hate loose ends, and this has just boggled my mind for years, much to my wife's chagrin. She says I think more about the missing woman than I do about her." Gil could relate to this man's plight. He chuckled.

"Incidentally," Ed Patterson continued, "one of the men they nabbed confessed to killing a woman near Joplin and throwing her out of the car. If she's still alive, that fellow went to the gas chamber for one crime he didn't commit. But who's going to quibble?" he chuckled.

"Is there a way I could get in touch with her husband?"

"He's in a nursing home now. His life just crumbled around him after his wife disappeared, and he finally had to give up his pulpit. His son, Carl, runs a boat rental place just outside of Camdenton though. I see him every now and then and stop to jaw with him a while. We never talk about his mother."

"Do you suppose he'd talk to me?"

"It's hard to say. I'll give you his number, but if you want me to talk to him first, I'd be glad to do that. How about I have him call you himself? If he doesn't want to, I'll call you back and tell you."

Gil finished his conversation with the retired reporter and hung up. His family hovered nearby, waiting to hear the verdict.

"Does he think Mollie's his missing woman?" Tim asked.

"He doesn't know for sure, but everything about Mollie fits the woman he's been searching for all these years."

Gil wanted desperately to be able to reunite Mollie with her family. But if she wasn't the missing woman, then he'd be giving a few people hope where there was none. He stared at the telephone, hoping it would bring good news next time. Didn't Mollie have a right to know who she really was?

"Is someone going to be here in case I get a phone call from either Carl Norris or Ed Patterson?"

"I'll be here, Dad," Tim told him. "Boyd is taking Mom's van to get a tree, and then we'll get it put up. I'll let you know if anyone calls."

"Boyd is dropping me back at the hospital," Pam told him. "So far there's been nothing new in Mollie's condition, and no one is doing much. I want to be there if someone does come to a conclusion."

They all sat down to eat their sandwiches, and Gil realized that he was ravenous. Good news, or maybe just better news, could make a guy really hungry.

"I may join you at the hospital if we're not too busy this afternoon. I won't be able to keep my mind on business anyhow." Like Ed Patterson, Gil also hated loose ends.

14

The first thing Gil saw that afternoon, when he opened the door to Mollie's hospital room, was the oxygen mask covering her nose and mouth and intravenous bottles dispensing medication through clear plastic tubes attached to Mollie's arm. He glanced at Pam who sat in a chair near Mollie's bed. A nurse, and a doctor Gil recognized, stood at the foot of Mollie's bed and were involved in a discussion. Before Gil could speak, Pam got up and motioned him back through the door into the hallway.

"Dr. Parker is really upset," Pam explained. "Evidently, Mollie wasn't examined properly last night when she was brought into the emergency room. No one realized she has pneumonia and has had it for quite some time, plus a concussion and the obvious contusions."

Gil stared in disbelief. "Why wasn't she examined?"

"Someone thought that since she was probably without funds, the hospital wouldn't want to foot the bill. Dr. Parker thinks differently. He's been ordering nurses and orderlies around ever since he arrived."

"Is Mollie still unconscious?"

"Yes, and she's having terrible nightmares, Gil. She whimpers like a wounded animal, and she keeps trying to throw off all the apparatus that's attached to her. She seems to be terrified of everything."

"Maybe she is. Being attacked last night, that alone could give her nightmares. But if she's the woman who disappeared over forty years ago after someone tried to murder her...no wonder she's terrified."

"Do you really think Mollie is that missing woman?"

"It sure seems to fit with what Duke told me."

"Just think! She'd finally be reunited with her family. No more eating out of dumpsters or sleeping in moldy hotels."

"That is *if* her family wants to be reunited with her," Gil said sadly.

"Gil, surely her sons would be longing to know what happened to their mother. They're both mature men now."

"Let's hope Carl Norris calls back. He seems to be our only link right now."

"Something good has to come of this." Pam shook her head sadly. "Tim feels so bad that Mollie was victimized. He blames himself."

"I don't blame Tim as much as I do myself," Gil said. "If I hadn't made such an issue of looking for Mollie, Tim never would have pointed Mollie out to Bailey Nickerson."

"Remember, there could be a miracle in this. Dr. Parker told me that Mollie has been battling pneumonia for almost a month. Without help, she would have eventually died on the street. Now, at least, she's getting some medical help."

"Did you get the necessary papers all signed?" Gil asked, suddenly remembering he'd left that task up to Pam.

"I did. And we have full responsibility for Mollie's hospital bill unless the hospital can come up with some source of funding for the expenses. The gal in administration said there are sources available. She's going to check on them for us."

"How does it feel to have adopted a bag lady?" Gil snickered.

Pam grimaced. "What if she needs a place to recuperate, Gil? Are we going to take her home with us?"

"We can't put her back on the street, can we?"

"No, of course not. I just keep thinking of all the crawly things that may be in her hair." Pam shivered at the thought.

"I'm sure they'll take care of any of that stuff while she's in the hospital. She'll be clean and polished by the time she leaves here." He smiled at his wife. "Don't you think so?" He leaned over and put his arm around her shoulder.

Just then the nurse came out of Mollie's room.

"Let's see if we can talk to Dr. Parker before he leaves." Gil headed into Mollie's room and went to stand by her bed. Dr. Parker knew who he was, but he introduced Pam to the doctor.

"How is she doing, Doctor?" Gil asked.

"Actually, not too bad for all she's been through. This old lady's a fighter. Even with the pneumonia followed by a pretty brutal beating, she's hanging on. The wound to her head was severe, and the concussion isn't good, but all the tests are okay. There doesn't seem to be any permanent damage. I expect her to wake up soon."

"We think she's had amnesia for over forty years. Is it possible that when she wakes up she might know who she is?"

"Since I'm not sure a person could have amnesia for that long, I'm not sure what her mind will be like when she wakes up. I did notice the horrible scar on her throat. If she was maimed that badly, it could have definitely affected her memory. Is she a relative, Mr. Hayworth?"

"No, just someone I've taken an interest in, and now look where my curiosity got me." Gil laughed.

"It never hurts to care about someone like Mollie, Mr. Hayworth. Especially someone as lonely as this woman must be. I can't imagine living on the streets, being prey to all the evil that lurks out there."

Gil leaned over Mollie's bed, and, not knowing why he did it, he started singing "Happy Birthday to You" softly in his deep baritone voice.

They were all startled when Mollie's eyes popped opened, and she looked at Gil. "Sonny?" She tried to whisper. "Is that you, Sonny?"

"Mollie, it's me. Gil Hayworth. Remember, you called me last night after you'd been hurt."

"I can't see you, Sonny. Where are you?

Pam tugged at Gil's sleeve. "Look at her eyes. She's not really awake."

The doctor went to check her eyes with his little pocket light and agreed. "No, she isn't awake, but the song must have triggered something. Do you know who Sonny is?

"He could be her son." Gil explained his earlier phone conversation with Ed Patterson and the mother disappearing just before her son's tenth birthday.

The doctor seemed encouraged by that news.

"She's evidently remembering something. It's possible the blow to her head has restored her memory, but right now, she needs to rest. Later on, though, I would encourage you to talk to her with facts about her past. The information might just trigger something in her brain."

After the doctor left, Pam sat down by Mollie's bed and held her hand. "She seems to be resting better now," Pam told him. "Maybe we should just leave her alone and let her sleep."

As much as Gil hated to leave Mollie alone in the hospital, he knew Pam was right, and nothing they did was going to help her get better. She'd have to do that by herself.

*****

At home, everything seemed to be under control. To Gil and Pam's amazement, the Christmas tree was upright in front of the large bay window, and Traci and Tim were busy trimming it. Tim kept one eye on the tree and one eye on the football game he was watching on TV. They found Boyd in the kitchen, popping popcorn for everyone. The dishes from lunch had all been cleaned up and put away, and much to Gil and Pam's dismay, the house looked festive and tidy. Knowing all this "togetherness" might not last much longer, they savored the moment and dug into Boyd's huge bowl of popcorn.

"How's Mollie?" Tim asked, just as the fourth quarter was ending. He plopped down on the couch, his tree trimming obviously finished.

"Doing pretty well," Gil told him. "She's even asking about someone named Sonny."

"Maybe that knock on the head wasn't all bad then," Boyd said, but Tim shook his head. "It was totally unnecessary," he said.

Gil saw that it was nearly three o'clock—five o'clock in Missouri. Carl Norris hadn't called. "I wonder if I should call Ed Patterson again."

Pam knew Gil wouldn't be happy unless he made that call. "Why don't you? You can ask him who Sonny is."

Gil dialed the number, and Mrs. Patterson answered and immediately turned the phone over to her husband. Perhaps, Gil thought, if Mollie is the missing woman, Ed Patterson's wife will finally be free of the "other woman" in her life.

Ed Patterson came on the line.

"Did you happen to talk to Carl Norris?" Gil asked.

"Naw. I called, but no luck. He may be at his daughter's in Sedalia. She's expecting a baby any day now."

"Is that a long trip from where you live?" Gil was unfamiliar with Missouri locales.

"Could be in this blizzard we're having back here. Carl and his wife may just decide to stay in Sedalia for a few days. His boat business is closed right now anyhow, so he wouldn't have any reason to stay home."

Gil's heart sank. "What about the other brother? Do you have his phone number?"

"'Fraid there isn't one, Mr. Hayworth. Ken died of polio two years after his mother left. It tore the old man up really bad. Carl is still bitter about Ken's death, blaming his absent mother. He blames her for everything that's ever happened to that family."

Gil felt a pang of sorrow for Mollie. If she was indeed the missing woman, she didn't even know her eldest son had died, and she'd never seen her youngest son's children. She was about to miss the joy of being a great-grandmother. What a waste of a precious life!

"Do you know if she called either of her sons Sonny?"

"I don't recall hearing anything like that. You'd have to ask Carl when you get in touch with him."

"Thanks, Mr. Patterson. I guess I'm at a dead end right now." Gil couldn't keep the discouragement out of his voice.

"I know what that feels like, Mr. Hayworth, but your call this morning opened up all kinds of new possibilities. For the first time in years, I feel good about this whole tragic business. I'll keep trying to reach Carl. Maybe you should try him too. One of us might connect." Gil thanked the elderly reporter for his help and hung up.

Gil wondered if what they were doing was really good for Mollie. Even if her memory returned, would she be able to comprehend all that has happened in the last forty years? What if her husband and son refused to forgive her? She might not be able to forgive them. After all, they never searched for her.

"I sure hope someone finds that fellow pretty soon," Tim said, breaking into Gil's thoughts.

"I hope so, too, Tim. If it were me in Mollie's old army boots, I'd be grateful to anyone who cared enough to try and find my family. Perhaps Mollie will feel the same way. Please, please, let it be so," Gil prayed, fervently.

15

Early Sunday morning, Gil tried to call Carl Norris, himself, but there was still no answer. Disappointed and too restless to sit while he waited for his family to get ready for church, he drove downtown to the Union Gospel Mission, hoping to find Duke. The old fellow needed to know what had happened to Mollie.

Much to Gil's relief, and probably to the relief of nearly everyone in Grayport, the spell of frigid air had broken, and the rain had returned. But the thaw combined with the rain now brought flood warnings to the area. As Gil drove along River Street, he saw how close the river was to overflowing its banks. If Mollie was still at the Grand Hotel, she'd soon have water lapping at her rear escape route. He was thankful that at least she was warm and safe where she was.

At the rescue mission, Gil found Duke washing breakfast dishes in the small but functional kitchen. Gil's first thoughts were of how weary Duke looked for so early in the day.

"I wanted to come by and tell you about Mollie," Gil said.

"I already know." Duke nodded sadly. "I been at the hospital all night."

"You have?" Gil had underestimated the speed of street information. He was sorry he hadn't told Duke sooner himself. "How was she when you were there?"

Duke shook his head. "Unconscious the whole time. She was having awful dreams. I tried to talk to her, but it didn't help."

"Duke, we think we may know who Mollie is. Can you come sit down with me so I can tell you about it?"

Duke looked at the pile of dishes and back at Gil. "I can't be too long but come on." He dried his hands and led the way to the dining room where a few men were still finishing their breakfast. They sat down at the end of one of the long tables.

Gil proceeded to tell Duke all that they'd learned from Ed Patterson. Duke nodded, his excitement growing with each new revelation. "Yep! Yep! It could be her, Mr. Hayworth," he said when Gil had finished. "Here I thought she was some gangster's girlfriend," Duke said sadly. "I should have insisted on findin' out where she came from."

"How would you have known where to look, Duke? You've been a good friend to Mollie, and you've taken good care of her. Her family will appreciate that, I'm certain."

Duke sat up straight, suddenly alarmed by something. "Mr. Hayworth, you say she may have been a preacher's wife?" He covered his face with his hands. "What if I'd done what I tried to do?"

Gil stared at the man. "What did you try to do, Duke?"

"You know. Her bein' a woman and me bein' a man and all. You know what I mean, Mr. Hayworth. Do you suppose the Lord will forgive me for tryin'?"

Gil chuckled and patted Duke on the shoulder. "You say nothing happened, and you didn't know who she was. Any red-blooded male traveling with an attractive female would have tried the same thing. I'm sure you're forgiven."

Duke wasn't easily mollified. "But I shoulda known she was no ordinary girl. I shoulda just known." He shook his head sorrowfully. "Now I just hope Mollie's tough enough to fight off bein' sick. She really needs to find her family."

"I know, Duke. More than anything, I want her to see her son again. If she's truly his mother, he'll want to see that she's properly cared for. Maybe he'll even want her to go back to Missouri with him."

Duke nodded in agreement although Gil could see that the thought saddened him. He'd miss looking out for her.

"I'll let you know just as soon as I talk to Carl Norris."

"Thanks, Mr. Hayworth. I 'preciate that."

"I've got to pick up my family now and go to church. Want to come along, Duke?"

The old man shook his head. "Naw. I get enough church here at the Mission. I'll just go finish up those dishes."

Gil was almost out the front door of the Mission when Duke called to him. "I forgot to tell you, Mr. Hayworth. When Mollie wakes up, she can talk to you if you know how to sign."

"Sign? You mean like a deaf person?"

"Yeah. We took classes together once a long time ago, so she can usually tell you how she's feelin' 'bout things. Sometimes you might not even want to know." He chuckled.

Gil was elated. Traci could sign. She'd had a class in school. It might be enough to actually be able to get Mollie to talk to them when she wakes up.

"Thanks, Duke. That's a big help. See you later." He waved as he went out the door.

While Duke scrubbed pots and pans, Gil sat with his family in a pew at the church, trying to keep his mind on the advent service. Gil and Pam had joined this small Presbyterian church before any of the children were born, and they'd worshipped there ever since. Gil usually had no problem listening to the pastor's message, but today it was hard to keep his mind focused. Instead he prayed for Mollie, prayed for the man back in Missouri who thought his wife had left him for another man. He prayed for Carl Norris and prayed that a phone call would come soon.

At the end of the service, Dr. Brooks, their young pastor, shook hands with Gil and reminded him of the Christmas program later that afternoon, the program in which Traci had a part. Gil's conscience nagged him as he left the church with his family. He'd forgotten about the Christmas pageant just as he'd forgotten everything else lately that had to do with his children. He couldn't shortchange Traci again. Mollie would never even know, much less care, whether he was at the hospital or not. He promised himself right then and there that when the family left for the program later, he'd be with them, his mind on his daughter's performance.

Gil and Pam ate lunch at home with the family and then prepared to make a quick visit to the hospital. "We'll be back in time to get you to the church, and after the program," Gil said, "I will treat the whole family to dinner out." He looked at Traci. "How's that?"

She grinned at her dad, no longer ashamed of her braces. After all, a boy had accepted her with them. Now she could accept herself too.

As Gil and Pam started out the door, Tim reminded him that he hadn't tried to call Carl Norris. Gil glanced at his watch. "I'll call him this evening, Tim."

But by the look of disappointment on Tim's face, Gil realized that wasn't what Tim wanted to hear. "Okay, I'll try the number again." He picked up the phone and dialed the number, his family all gathered around him in the study. To his surprise, a man's deep voice answered on the third ring.

"Mr. Norris, my name's Gil Hayworth, and I live in Grayport, Washington. I may have some information about your mother that may shock you." When the man didn't respond, Gil continued, "Mr. Norris, we have reason to believe that she is here in Grayport."

"I believe you're mistaken, Mr. Hasbrook," the man snapped. "My mother couldn't be in Washington State."

"Why not? Do you know where she is?"

"My mother ran off and left her family forty-three years ago last May, on my birthday in fact, and we haven't heard from her since. If she's decided now that she wants to come home, she's out of luck."

"Mr. Norris, she doesn't want to come home. She doesn't even know who she is. She's had amnesia for over forty years."

"Do you really believe that, Mr. Hasbrook? I think someone is pulling your leg."

"My name is Hayworth, and even Ed Patterson thinks this woman could be the one he's searched for all these years. Did she ever call you or your brother Sonny?"

There was a heavy silence on the other end of the line. Gil thought Carl Norris had hung up. "Mr. Norris? Are you there?"

A quieter voice answered, "Yes, I'm here."

"Mr. Norris, she's been severely beaten and is still unconscious in the hospital. She came around once and whispered for someone named Sonny. She can't talk much. Someone cut her vocal cords years ago and left her to bleed to death."

"I don't know any Sonny," the man snarled. "Please, don't bother me again." The phone went dead in Gil's ear.

Gil sat down heavily in the desk chair, shocked at what he'd just heard. The man had no feelings. Sure, he'd been hurt, and Gil could understand the bitterness, but wasn't he curious enough to want to find out for sure? "I almost hope he isn't Mollie's son. She doesn't deserve someone like him in her life."

"Gil," Pam put her arm around him, "I'm sure if he understood, he'd care. He was just a small boy when she disappeared. Little boys pretend all sorts of things to make the hurt go away. And maybe his father filled his head with lies about her. He's just removed her from existence."

"But she does exist, Pam, and someone has to care about her."

"You do. I do. Our kids do. Duke does. Maybe that's all she's going to have. And maybe Carl Norris will change his mind."

"Maybe Ed Patterson will talk him into listening."

*****

Gil was still upset with Carl Norris when he and Pam walked into Mollie's room at the hospital. The oxygen mask had been removed, but all the tubes were still connecting Mollie to her medication. Mollie was sleeping soundly. The sound of rain spattering the windows and dripping onto a roof below mingled with the sounds from the equipment attached to Mollie.

Gil leaned over the bed, listening to Mollie's faint breathing. "Are you ever going to wake up, Mary Margaret Norris?" He took her thin, white hand in his.

Mollie's eyes fluttered open, startling Gil, and focused on his face. "Sonny?"

"Mollie, it's me. Gil Hayworth. Do you remember me?"

She nodded her head slightly and turned to smile weakly at him. "You do remember me." He chuckled, elated. "How do you feel?" She gave no response, just watched him with watery blue eyes.

"Can you remember anything else, Mollie? You called me Sonny. Do you remember Sonny?" No reaction. She continued to stare at him.

"Mollie, do you remember Carl? How about Carl's tenth birthday party?" Gil's voice was getting louder with each question, and Pam sensed the desperation that drove him. She took his arm and pulled him away from the bed.

"Gil, it's no use," Pam said. "She's exhausted." Mollie's eyes had closed again. "Come on," Pam coaxed. "Let's go get a cup of coffee and let her rest."

Gil's tense muscles relaxed some as he followed Pam out of the room. She was right. Mollie was exhausted and might never regain the strength she needed to recover. Gil didn't want to think about her dying without knowing who she really was.

*****

Mollie heard them leave the room, but she was too tired to open her eyes. Every joint and muscle in her body ached, and any movement, no matter how small, was agony for her. She lay there, very still, her mind beginning to slowly function. Of course she could remember her small, tow-headed Sonny on his tenth birthday. Why did that fella ask such silly questions? And why did he call him Carl? She'd forgotten Sonny's candles. What a stupid thing to do! She'd have to run to the store...but she was so tired.

Mollie dozed. When she awoke, shadows filled the room. She moved her head slightly, and pain tore at her skull. When the pain subsided, she could see the dark clouds through the window and rain lashed against the glass. Rain! She hated the rain. But at least it was warmer when it rained. She hated those cold, bitter days even more than the rain.

She tried to move her head again. *Where are my boots and my warm coat?* she thought. *I'll be needin' 'em when I get outta here. I hope nobody's lost 'em. You can find more clothes, but a good coat and boots are hard to find.* She moved her head again and waited for the pain to subside. What was she going to do now? She couldn't go back to the hotel now that those mean kids knew she lived there. She couldn't ask Duke to move on. She'd promised herself that she wouldn't do that again. Maybe she'd have to go alone. She couldn't stay in this town any longer.

Those darned kids! she said to herself. *They hit my head and now I think weird stuff.* Brief flashes of familiar faces danced through her memory, and the image of a man in a long, black robe shaking his fist at her frightened her. Mollie knew she was full of sin. The man in the robe had told her that. She liked to sleep bare naked. She liked Elvis Presley's music, and she liked watching the rock-and-roll king gyrate on their tiny television set. She liked to paint her fingernails and toenails with the brightest red polish. *Oh, Avery, let me be,* she pleaded with the man in the robe. *I ain't hurtin' no one.*

Mollie's eyes flew open. She suddenly knew who Avery was. He was her husband, the father of her two boys. *Where were the boys?* She had to find her boys. She tried to move again, but the pain was too intense. She sobbed, nearly choking herself. What if Avery found out what those awful men did to her? He'd never forgive her. *Avery, I didn't want them to do it...* Mollie struggled to sit up, but the pain forced her back down on the bed. She heard someone scream, heard people running in the halls, then she passed out.

The nurses had heard the scream and ran up and down the hall, searching for the source, never suspecting that Mollie was capable of making such a terrifying sound. When they glanced into her room, they thought she was asleep.

"Couldn't be her," one of them said. "She can't talk."

They went back to their tasks, still puzzling over the scream they'd all heard, but no patient to go with it.

16

After some time in the coffee shop with Pam, Gil decided to leave the hospital and drive downtown to the police station. He wanted to ask Chief Burgess if he'd had any success in arresting Mollie's attackers. When the chief wasn't in his office, Gil approached the young, uniformed woman at the front desk.

"Do you know if the men who attacked the bag lady Friday night have been caught?"

"You must be Mr. Hayworth." She smiled at him. "Chief Burgess said you'd be inquiring about Mollie. We do have two suspects in custody. One has confessed to being at the hotel, but he says he didn't do the beating. The other man refuses to talk."

"Can you give me their names?"

"I'm afraid not, Mr. Hayworth. You'd have to talk to the chief for that information."

Gil nodded, understanding, and turned to leave.

"How is Mollie doing?" the young officer asked.

"Not very well. The cold weather and the beating has taken a toll on her."

"I'm sorry to hear that. Mollie is a favorite of ours. After all, she's Grayport's only bag lady, and there's something special about her. Funny, isn't it? When I saw her on the street the first time, I just wanted to go home and give my grandmother a big hug, so grateful that she didn't lead a life like Mollie's."

"I know. She does have a way of getting one's attention." Gil thought of his own pursuit of the old woman.

"And our weather makes you wonder why anyone would choose Grayport to spend the winter on the streets. Seattle would be bad enough, but at least they provide some shelter for their street people."

"I guess the place looked good when they arrived, she and her friend Duke. He says they thought they'd found a warm, coastal haven."

"And we're having the coldest winter in two decades. Poor Mollie!"

Gil turned to leave. "Will you have the chief contact me at the drugstore tomorrow?"

"I'll tell him, Mr. Hayworth."

Back at the hospital, Gil pulled up a chair and joined Pam at Mollie's bedside. The gray Sunday afternoon dragged slowly by with only hospital sounds and the splattering of rain against the window to keep them company. They both knew they'd have to leave the hospital by four o'clock to be able to get Traci to the church in time for the pageant at five. Gil also knew that Mollie's condition was unlikely to change, but still he hated to leave her alone. Maybe Duke would be back before they left, then Gil wouldn't mind leaving so much.

Suddenly the quiet was broken as Tim and Boyd bounded into the room.

"Guess what, Dad?" Tim tried to whisper but was too excited to succeed. "Boyd just talked to Carl Norris."

"What?" Gil couldn't believe his ears. "He called us?"

"Yeah, Dad," Boyd put in. "He says to tell you he's really sorry about the way he talked to you earlier. Evidently, Ed Patterson paid him a visit later, after you'd talked to him, and laid out the whole chain of events for Mr. Norris. He says now that you could be right about Mollie being his mother."

Gil's heart was pounding in his chest. He glanced over at Mollie, still sleeping soundly despite the commotion in her room.

"Yeah, Dad, they're *both* coming to Grayport," Tim told him.

Gil still couldn't believe what he was hearing. "How soon will that be?"

"They have no idea," Boyd explained. "There are no planes taking off from St. Louis because of the snowstorm, and they have to get from Camdenton to St. Louis first anyhow. He says the roads are terrible. They'll come just as soon as the weather clears enough and planes can take off."

"But what if Mollie's not his mother? He'll have wasted his time and money."

"Mr. Norris admitted that his mother always called him Sonny, never Carl. He's pretty sure she's his mother and so is Mr. Patterson."

Tears poured down Gil's face, and before long they were all weeping with happiness. "Mollie's finally going to be vindicated with her family," Gil said, breathing easier.

"One of them will call you when they make it to St. Louis and can catch a flight to Seattle. I told them someone would be there to meet them when they arrived in Seattle," Boyd told his dad.

"Thanks, son. This is all good news." He glanced toward the door.

"Where's Traci? Why didn't she come with you?"

"She did." Tim laughed. "But one of the nurses stopped her in the hall and said she was too young to be visiting on this floor. Can you believe it?"

"Yeah," Boyd continued, "she's down on the main floor, in the waiting room by the nurses' station. She wants to talk to you, Dad, when you get a chance."

"Sounds serious," Gil said. "Maybe I'd better go down and talk to her. Anyone else coming with me?"

"Go ahead, Gil," Pam told him, "we'll wait here with Mollie."

Gil found Traci in the waiting room, thumbing through a magazine. Somehow she looked older today even though she still wore the same blue jeans and baggy yellow sweater she'd had on after church. As he approached, she looked up and smiled, her braces gleaming. Her short, curly hair framed her small face, and Gil thought she was beautiful, just like her mother.

"What's up, Trace? The guys said you wanted to talk to me. Did they ask you about signing when Mollie wakes up?"

"Yeah, they told me, Dad, and I'll be glad to do that if the nurses will let me in her room. But that's not why I wanted to see you. I just want to tell you that you and Mom don't have to go to the Christmas pageant tonight." Gil opened his mouth to object, but Traci stopped him. "Dad, it's not as though you've missed any of my programs. I've never been neglected. I'll be fourteen in two months, and assuming they didn't use me as the Baby Jesus when I was tiny, you've sat through at least twelve or thirteen Christmas pageants. The story hasn't changed, you know. It's the same now as it always has been." She grinned impishly, her green eyes sparkling. "I know you're worried about Mollie. So am I. Stay here with her." She hugged him. "Besides you wouldn't have your mind on the program anyhow."

Gil peered into Traci's eyes, trying to determine if she was in one of her "moods" but decided that she wasn't. At that moment, he was so proud of his daughter. "Traci, we're going to the pageant if we can, but you're right, my mind won't totally be on it. I'm sorry I haven't paid much attention to your life lately, the dance, your boyfriend, school stuff."

"That's okay, Dad. Boyd and Tim are going to the pageant and will try not to look too bored. I'm a big angel this year, and you would never believe that anyhow." She smiled, her braces shining.

"Oh, I don't know. You're a very special angel to me right now." He hugged her tightly. "And Trace," he grinned, sheepishly, "you were the Baby Jesus when you were tiny. Your mother and I were Mary and Joseph."

Traci shook her head. "Somehow that doesn't surprise me." She laughed.

After Boyd, Tim, and Traci left the hospital, Pam started planning for the visitors from Missouri. "If they can get here next week, there's no school. The kids will be a big help."

"You wouldn't have said that a month ago."

"You know, you're right. Mollie has affected all of us. For once, our children are pulling together instead of being at each other's throats. Anyhow, I must call Hank and tell him we won't be at their house for Christmas."

"Pam! You don't want to give up being with your family over the holidays. We can still go to Hank's house."

"We can't expect our two visitors to fend for themselves especially if they've never been to Washington State before. And I wouldn't feel right inviting them to Hank's. He'll have a crowd of people as it is."

Gil shook his head. "I just hate for you to change all your plans."

"Gil, I'm not complaining. Besides if Mollie gets to feeling well enough, she might be released from the hospital to spend Christmas at our house."

Gil couldn't believe his ears. This was the same woman who didn't want him wasting time on a dirty old bag lady. "I've really started something, haven't I, Pam?"

"You mean when you got involved with Mollie? You sure did. Your curiosity is bigger than anyone else's I know, but so is your heart. Why do you think I love you so much?"

"You say that now," he grinned, "but you'll be mad at me again when you realize you aren't getting a Christmas present. Actually no one is getting a Christmas present. I haven't done any shopping yet."

"You know what, Gil? There's still time, and you're not going to use Mollie as an excuse." She cocked one eye at him. "There had better be presents," she threatened.

17

The call from St. Louis came at nine o'clock on Tuesday morning. Gil had just opened the drugstore and was sorting through the answering machine messages when Pam called from home to tell him.

Gil had spent an edgy Monday trying to concentrate on drugstore business while waiting for the call from Carl Norris. Gil learned that Duke had spent most of Monday at Mollie's bedside, trying to get her to wake up and talk to him. But he'd had no success. Mollie had roused a couple of times, called out names unfamiliar to Duke, and then slipped back in unconsciousness.

School vacation had begun on Monday much to the delight of everyone.

Pam and Traci had finally finished their shopping. Traci was proud of her Christmas purchases, even buying something for Duke and for Mollie until she found out Tim and Boyd had had the same idea. Duke and Mollie would be the proud owners of three pair of knitted gloves each and three knitted ski caps each. Fortunately, they were all different, so Duke and Mollie would have a nice variety.

On Tuesday, Pam and Traci had planned on baking their traditional Christmas cookies. Boyd had promised to make his infamous fudge after he finished his shift at the service station that afternoon. His winter hours were limited, so he tried to squeeze in work whenever there was an opportunity. He needed to add to his bank account if he wanted that newer car. Tim had promised to get his and Boyd's bedroom in shape for the Missouri visitors which Pam feared might take some doing.

Gil was relieved when Pam called. "There's a flight leaving for Seattle in forty minutes," Pam told him. "They plan to be on that plane," she repeated what Carl Norris had told her. "He and Ed

Patterson made it to St. Louis early this morning and learned that the airport had reopened even though the roads were still treacherous. He's worried that they're making this trip for nothing, Gil."

"I'm sure he is. I'll admit I've had a few shaky moments worrying about their trip myself, Pam. But we can't dwell on that now. Those two men are probably getting on that plane now as we speak. I'll be home in a few minutes." Knowing Boyd was working, he added, "maybe Tim would like to ride to Seattle with me. If I take your van, we'll have plenty of room."

"Mr. Norris suggested they just rent a car, but I told him you were planning to meet them at the airport."

"Good. Jeanne's already here, and she's been briefed on the situation, so the store is in good hands. I'll be home shortly."

Gil left immediately for home. The rain had stopped again, and the sun was poking through the thinning clouds, making the day a pleasant one for the moment. If it stayed nice, the drive to SeaTac Airport would be tolerable. But the weather could change at any moment. One of the favorite sayings on the harbor was "Don't like the weather? Wait an hour and it'll change." Gil was inclined to think that could happen on the two-hour drive to Seattle.

At home, Tim was ready and waiting, obviously glad to get out of cleaning his bedroom. Boyd would be faced with that task, too, when he got home from work.

Gil chuckled. "Don't forget! Boyd has to make his infamous fudge too. Can't have Christmas without it!"

The trip to Seattle went by quickly, partly because Gil and Tim had a good opportunity to talk about all the things they seldom talked about—school, football, his grades, Bailey Nickerson. Tim still hadn't forgiven himself for getting Mollie into trouble even though Gil explained that if it hadn't been Bailey Nickerson who beat up on her, eventually it would have been some other Grayport thug.

They also discussed Tim's car troubles, his college hopes, his girlfriend, and the Missouri visitors. Tim, like Gil, was concerned about what trauma Carl Norris's appearance would cause Mollie.

At the airport, Gil parked the car on the fourth level of the enclosed, spiral parking lot, and he and Tim walked through a glass-enclosed walkway over a busy thoroughfare to get inside the airport. Once in the huge lobby, television monitors overhead told them the gate number of the St. Louis flight. They rode two escalators, went through the metal detectors, and then rode the underground tram to the satellite building where their visitors would be arriving. They still had some time before the plane arrived, and tension was mounting in both Gil and Tim.

"How will we know these guys?" Tim asked as he eyed a pretty teenage girl that passed by with her family.

"I'm not sure," Gil answered. "I guess we just look for someone who's looking for someone." He hadn't really planned the next step. He would take it one step at a time. What they were trying to do would either bring great joy or great disaster. Gil prayed it wouldn't be the latter.

As they sat waiting, several announcements were made for flight cancellations across the country due to weather conditions. Passengers trying to get out of Seattle and on to their holiday destinations mumbled their vexation. People waiting for family and friends that weren't going to arrive were equally vexed. Gil watched the monitor for the flight arriving from St. Louis. The arrival time had not changed, much to Gil's relief.

Gil and Tim ate sandwiches at a small restaurant down the corridor from their gate and browsed through the gift shop next door to the restaurant, killing time until the announcement came that the flight from St. Louis was arriving. On a distant runway, a 747 touched down, and within minutes, the gleaming silver aircraft was taxiing toward the airport. As they waited for the two men to disembark, Gil became more and more anxious. He and Tim searched for two faces that might be their visitors, then Gil discovered that no search was necessary. A man peering through the throng of passengers, looking directly at Gil, looked exactly like Mollie. Though he was a much younger version, his face was the same weathered face with the same blue eyes and narrow, pointed chin. Gil pushed through the crowd and offered his hand to Carl Norris.

"How did you know who I was?" the man asked.

"Believe it or not, you look like your mother."

Carl Norris stared at him. "You're sure about that?"

"No doubt whatsoever!"

As soon as they moved into a less crowded area, they stopped to introduce each other around. Gil sensed the bitterness in Mollie's slightly overweight, balding son, but he accepted it for now. Ed Patterson was a slow talker with a heavy Missouri drawl. Gil liked him immediately. Neither man exuded signs of wealth because both men's overcoats showed signs of wear and tear. Gil smiled, remembering Ed Patterson's wife and her shrill voice on the telephone. She must have many other redeeming qualities that kept the tall, wiry man married to her. Her voice would have sent Gil over the edge long ago.

They reversed the tram trip, two escalators rides, and passed several food vendors on the way back to the main terminal. Gil asked the men about needing to eat, but they declined. They retrieved the one suitcase for each man, crossed the bridge to parking, and left the airport. On the drive out of Seattle, Ed Patterson, in the back seat with Tim, noted the green trees and grass.

"I can't believe how lush and green everything looks in December. Wish I could stay long enough to see some of your scenery."

"How long can you stay?" Gil asked.

"Only long enough to make arrangements for getting my mother, if indeed she is my mother, back home," Carl Norris told him.

"It may be a while before she can travel," Gil explained. "She's really ill right now, and don't forget her years with amnesia. She doesn't remember anything before being in the hospital in Joplin, and trying to move her too soon might cause her some painful trauma."

"I'm aware of that, Mr. Hayworth, but the airline people assure me that arrangements can be made to fly my mother safely back to Missouri." The man's coldness troubled Gil. Doesn't he feel anything for his mother?

"But it's too soon. Maybe when she's recovered some..."

"What is your real interest in her, Mr. Hayworth? Don't expect any money because we don't have any."

Gil bristled. In the rearview mirror, he saw Ed Patterson's surprise and the shake of his head, maybe trying to warn Gil away from the subject.

"I'm only interested in Mollie for Mollie's sake. She's been through a lot lately, and I care what happens to her."

"There are thousands of street people across the country, Mr. Hayworth, but very few of them would claim to have amnesia as a reason to run out on their families."

"You think she's faking the amnesia?"

"It's hard to believe otherwise, Mr. Hayworth. I was only ten years old when she left, but I was old enough to know that my father's rigid rules and his strict Southern Baptist ministry were hard on her. I believe she just decided that night to escape and didn't give one thought to the two little kids she was leaving behind."

"Mr. Patterson suspected she'd met with foul play. Why didn't you listen to him?" Gil persisted.

"Members of my father's congregation had warned him not to marry her because they thought she had loose morals. He loved her too much to give her up, so he married her against all their objections. When she left, they convinced him that they'd been right all along."

"No one ever considered she might be in danger?"

"When Ed suggested that she might have met up with those three killers, my father preferred to think she'd gone off with another man. Besides, there was never any trace of her."

"And what did you boys think? Didn't you trust her enough to think she wouldn't do something like that?"

"My brother and I had no opinion in the matter. Since we'd helped Ma keep secrets from Pa on several occasions, it was easy to believe that this was another one of her secrets." Carl Norris smiled, surprising Gil. "She used to paint her toenails bright red and then hide them in her shoes all day, smiling a smug little smile. She painted Kenny's toes, too, but he hated it. I always liked it when she painted mine. It made me feel closer to her, like we shared a special secret. She also like to listen to Elvis Presley and would dance all over the house to his music on the radio. Pa knew she liked Elvis, but she never danced when he was around. One day, she also told us some other things Pa disapproved of, but we were so embarrassed by what she said we tried to put it out of our minds. She said she liked to sleep naked, and she loved long, luxurious bubble baths. She also told us that Pa lived in fear that someone in the congregation would find out. Kenny and I could never figure out why the bubble baths would be sinful, but we sure understood about the naked part."

"You never told on her about the nail painting?"

"No, I guess we enjoyed time away from Pa's strict rules as much as she did."

Gil remembered Duke's description of the woman who had climbed on that westbound freight. Even without makeup and in need of medical help, Duke had thought she was beautiful. It wasn't hard to picture her with her two young sons as they went about their furtive toenail painting."

"So she did love you?"

"We had always thought so. It was just hard to understand why she'd go off and leave us. We thought maybe we'd done something to make her mad at us, but after hearing all the talk and getting fingers pointed at us, we started thinking as our pa did, that she was the bad one."

"What happened to your brother?" Gil asked.

"We had a polio epidemic the year after my mother left, and somehow Ken contracted bulbar polio. We'd been warned to stay away from swimming pools and large groups of people, but that was no problem for Kenny and me. We never went anywhere anyhow. We never knew where he picked up the disease, but he was in an iron lung for weeks. Kenny was Camdenton's first and only death from polio."

"He was older than you?"

"Yes. He was thirteen when he died."

"Gil felt the pain of grief for the small boy who'd first been abandoned by his mother and then by his brother. He wished he had the right words to say to Carl Norris, but none came. Still, he felt an even greater sadness for all Mollie had lost.

"And it was so unnecessary," Carl Norris commented.

"Your brother's death?"

"No, my mother's excuse that she needed candles for my birthday cake."

Gil felt a wave of despair. Why couldn't the man understand how important those candles would have been to a fun-loving mother? Her disappearance from his life was not *her* fault.

Traffic was heavy as they drove along Tacoma's four-lane freeway. Ed Patterson had added little to the conversation, his interests more on the scenery that Tim pointed out to him. Mount Rainier, with blue sky as a backdrop, was clearly visible now that the clouds had lifted, and the distant mountain shimmered in the winter sunlight.

"Everything looks freshly washed." Ed said. "Carl? Are you seeing any of this?" he asked his friend.

Carl Norris nodded that he was, but Gil knew the man's thoughts were elsewhere.

"I understand your father is in a nursing home. How is he?"

"Not very well. His mind is confused. When my mother left, he had his congregation's full support, so we got along pretty well. After Kenny died though, Pa's health went downhill fast. He blamed himself, his religion, he even blamed God for everything that had gone wrong in his life. He finally gave up his ministry, and after that, his mind wandered more and more."

"Did you tell him you were coming to Washington?"

"Yes, I did. I hoped the news might jar him out of his lethargy. He's just waiting to die."

"Maybe after you see your mother, you'll be able to convince him that she's alive."

"Maybe. If she's truly my mother, and if he can ever actually see her, he'll recognize her. I'm sure of that."

"Would you put Mollie in the nursing home with him?" Gil hated the idea and was pretty sure Mollie would too. She'd never be happy if she couldn't fend for herself and be independent.

"I'd have no other choice, Mr. Hayworth. There's no room anywhere else. I couldn't expect my wife or our kids to take care of her. I can't imagine that any of our children will be interested in knowing their grandmother is a bag lady."

"But what about Mollie? Doesn't she deserve something better after all these years?"

"If she's really my mother, then I owe her some security in her last years. I can't expect any of my family to love her right from the start, can I?"

Gil decided he'd had enough of the conversation. He listened as Tim narrated the scenic tour as they passed by the State Capitol dome in Olympia all the way to Grayport's rain-washed countryside. Daylight was beginning to fade by the time they arrived at the Hayworth driveway, and new clouds were bringing more drizzle in off the ocean. The two men who had just left snow and subfreezing temperatures behind them didn't object to the rain and the warmer climate. Ed Patterson was still marveling at Washington's beauty as he unloaded his suitcase from the back of the van and was still marveling in his slow Missouri drawl as Pam showed both men to the guest bedroom upstairs.

18

After the two men had rested and had enjoyed Pam's baked salmon dinner, Gil went with them to the hospital. Pam excused herself by saying she had some last-minute gift wrapping to do, but Gil suspected that she wanted to be absent when Carl Norris saw his mother for the first time in over forty years. Gil, on the other hand, was anxious to see the man's reaction. He didn't agree with Carl Norris's plan for Mollie's future, but Gil had the greatest hope that the doctor would also disapprove strongly of any changes in her lifestyle until she was well. And what about Mollie? Obviously she'd never flown before. She would be terrified.

In the hospital room, the three men quietly approached Mollie's bedside. Gil knew that the resemblance between Carl and his mother was unmistakable, but he was unprepared for the man's reaction when he walked up to the bed and looked at Mollie. He gasped and his shoulders began to shake violently as wracking sobs escaped his lips. Gil took him by one arm, and Ed Patterson took the other as they led him back out into the hall. There they found a chair and helped him into it. It was several minutes before he regained his composure and was finally able to look at Gil.

"You were right," he said shakily. "She is my mother." He took several deep breaths, wiping away the tears that streamed down his face. "My grandmother, my mother's mother, died about five years ago just before her ninetieth birthday," he told them. "Your Mollie and my grandmother could have been twins." The sobs began again. Gil kept his hand on the grieving man's shoulder. Through the tears, Carl Norris moaned, "What a horrid life she must have endured just because we didn't try to find her. How can I ever forgive myself for that?"

"You can," Gil tried to console him. "Her life has had some good years. You should talk to her friend, Duke, and let him tell you about the night he found her and all the places they've been since. Mollie has met some good people and some bad people. She hasn't been a bag lady for all those years."

Ed Patterson agreed with Gil. "You were only ten years old, Carl. You couldn't have searched for her. Where would you have looked? It was your father who should have insisted on looking. By the time you were old enough, too many other things crowded into your life, college, marriage, children, and your own boat building business."

Carl Norris shook his head sadly. "So many times I've wondered where she was. I never understood why she didn't want to see us. I think I wanted to see her just to tell her how much I hated her." He looked up at Gil, his face ashen. "Thank you for caring enough to find out who she really is and for finding me." He stood up and started toward the door to Mollie's room. "I want you both to stay with me," he said. "I want to talk to her. Maybe she'll remember me."

"If and when she responds, Duke tells me she can sign," Gil explained. "And our daughter can also. Maybe it would be easier for Mollie if Traci were with us."

"That is a good idea," Carl agreed. "If she responds at all, we'll bring your daughter with us tomorrow."

As they stood at Mollie's bedside, Gil was glad to see that much of the pent-up tension had gone out of Carl's body. Perhaps now he would reconsider any notion of taking Mollie back to Missouri with him. At least until she's more able to travel.

Gil leaned down over the bed. "Mollie," he said quietly. "Sonny's here to see you."

All three men were startled when Mollie's eyes fluttered open. She looked into her son's face. Carl spoke to her. "Ma, it's me Sonny. It's been such a long time. Do you remember me?"

"I just went out for candles," she tried to talk, but her voice was a low, gravely whisper. "Are your friends here yet?"

Tears welled up in Carl's eyes again. "Ma, the party's over, and the kids have all gone home." His shoulders began to shake again, Gil reached over to comfort him.

"There were no candles," she tried to tell him. "You had no candles." She tried repeatedly to talk to him. She seemed to forget that she couldn't speak.

"I had candles, Ma. There were several boxes in the drawer where you kept the napkins. We never understood why you went out to get more."

Suddenly Gil understood. That was why they'd thought she'd gone off with another man. She hadn't needed candles at all. They had believed it was just an excuse to leave.

Mollie stared up at him, her face drawn up, puzzled. "We did? I couldn't find them," she whispered coarsely. She kept her eyes on Carl's face as if she didn't really believe he could be Sonny.

"We were worried about you, Ma. You never came back."

She reached out and tried to pat his hand. "It's late," she said, barely understandable. "You boys better get to bed." She closed her eyes.

"You rest easy, Ma. Everything's going to be okay." He patted her hand and laid it gently down on the sheet. As Mollie drifted off to sleep, the men left the room, each emotionally drained.

In the hall, Ed Patterson said to Gil. "Guess I can put my forty-year search for Carl's mother to rest now." He glanced at Carl. "You know, I'm glad," he told him. "Even in my retirement years, I've never been able to get her out of my mind. I've always hoped and prayed that she'd turn up one day."

"I never did," Carl Norris admitted. "I never thought she'd show her face around us again. I have never told my wife or kids about what really happened, not all of it. My wife knows my mother left us, and she understands how I felt about her leaving. She was shocked when Ed told us she might have been found and even more shocked to learn that we had never tried to look for her."

As for Gil, everything seemed to be changing, and it made him sad. Even if Mollie stayed in Grayport, she would not be his responsibility any longer. Perhaps Carl would put her in a convalescent home until she was well enough to travel to Missouri. Gil would miss the trips to the Old Grand and his drives around town, searching for her. What would these men think if they knew he'd bought flowers for her musty old room at the hotel? They'd think the gesture had been as foolish as he, himself, thought now.

*****

After the men left the room, Mollie opened her eyes. She smiled to herself. She still had her knack for putting things over on people. How far gone did they think she was? Mr. Hayworth had pretended to be her friend, and now he was dragging middle-aged men into her room telling her he was her son. How ridiculous! Her son was only ten years old. Why were they trying to confuse her?

Mollie was glad her memory had returned. Behind her closed eyes, she could see the images of Avery and their two fine sons. Kenny was getting so tall, and now Sonny was turning ten years old. She'd have to do something special for him to make up for the absence of candles on his cake.

What had that man said? There were candles in a drawer? I always kept the candles up in a top cupboard. Why would he say something like that? Why would someone pretend to be someone he wasn't? What did that man want? Maybe he wanted to hurt me. Was he one of the men that hurt me? Mollie's frustration began to mount. Her mind wasn't working right. She couldn't think straight, and her body wouldn't work. Why couldn't she move?

She opened her eyes and looked at herself, lying in the bed. What was going on? Why was she in bed? *I gotta get out of here,* she thought to herself, but as she tried to move, she was overcome with blinding pain that flashed through her head. She reached up with one shaky hand and felt the bandage. Images crowded into her mind as she lay quietly, eyes closed to avoid the pain. Behind her eyelids she saw her sons. Then she saw Avery in his long, black robe. She loved Avery, and though he was morally strict, she wasn't afraid of him. He loved her, she knew, and he put up with so many of her silly antics because he loved her.

She could see Duke and the man who brought flowers. What were they doing with Avery? Mollie couldn't sort it all out. Nothing fit together anymore. She cried quietly at first, then as the memories began to flood her mind, she began to sob. Her past came together with the present, and Mollie remembered!

She remembered leaving the house that night, walking to the neighborhood grocery store for birthday candles. She began to shake with terror, remembering coming out of the little store and being grabbed by three men and being thrown into a car. She remembered fighting and clawing them with the long fingernails that Avery had only tolerated. She had managed to scratch all three of them before they were done with her. Still they succeeded in raping her, all three of them. She remembered the pain, the torturous pain before she passed out.

She reached up and rubbed the scar on her throat. How many years had she wondered about that scar, never able to remember what had happened to her. She had thought that maybe the man in the long, black robe had done it. Now she realized the men in the car had done it and left her beside the road to die. How she got to the hospital, she still didn't remember, or how she got out of the hospital. All she remembered after that was meeting up with Duke and their wild freight train travels headed west.

The sobs had ceased, and only gentle tears flowed as she relived the years in California, in Oregon, and then the last few months in Grayport. She could see Mr. Hayworth behind her closed eyes. She felt her whole soul smile.

He had brought her flowers, only flowers she'd ever had.

Then the memories started to be garbled once again, and Mollie panicked. *I have to find Avery,* she thought. *I have to explain to him what happened. What if he can't forgive me?*

Mollie opened her eyes, and in spite of the pain, she forced herself to move her eyes to look around the room. There was no one else there. One side rail on her bed had been left down, probably by someone who was coming back to poke and prod her sore body. If she could just sit up, getting out of bed shouldn't be too tough.

It took all the strength she could muster to grab the other side rail with both hands and pull herself into a sitting position. The effort left her exhausted, and pain coursed through her whole body, threatening to knock her down again. She sat upright for several minutes, holding on, taking deep breaths.

As soon as she could summon up more energy, she yanked the tubes out of her arms and threw them aside. She struggled to turn in the bed until her legs hung over the side. She waited another minute for the pain to subside, then she began stretching her toes, trying to touch the floor.

I can't wait no more, she told herself, and with one mighty surge of effort, she pushed herself off the bed and landed in a heap on the cold tile floor. Overwhelming pain engulfed her, but she refused to cry out. Instead, using her own bed for support, and with much grunting and moaning, she pulled herself up until she stood, stooped, by the bed. Purple spots and bright lights danced before her eyes. She prayed the dizziness would not cause her to fall or to pass out. She hung on tightly to the foot of the bed. After what seemed like an eternity, the dizziness passed, and she could breathe easier. *I must thank Mr. Hayworth,* she told herself.

She worked her way to the bedside table and opened the drawer. There was nothing there but hospital junk. Finally, she found a wadded-up paper with hospital rules on it. She smoothed it out, and, with a stubby pencil she found in the drawer, she scribbled a note on the back of the paper. She smiled remembering the phone numbers that Mr. Hayworth had written on the sack of sandwiches. That note had saved her life.

She propped the note up against a vase of real flowers on the bedside table, and then using the bed for support, then one chair, then another chair, then the sink near the door, then by grabbing the doorknob, she struggled through the open door into the hall. Her strength was nearly gone, but determination drove her on farther down the hall. No nurses were in sight, and the one man she could see couldn't see her. He was dozing in a chair by a patient's bed across the hall.

Mollie's feet seemed to get heavier as she made her way down the hall, using the wall for support. She looked down to be sure that she wasn't wearing her green rubber boots. She saw the stairway door just down the hall, but she'd have to cross the hall. Could she make it? She had to make it. She had to find Avery and tell him some bald-headed man was pretending to be Sonny. And where was Kenny? Had the bald-headed man done something to Kenny? Mollie saw the elevator doors, but she feared being seen if she tried to get into an elevator. The stairway would be safer. By the time she reached the stairway door, her strength was gone. She heard someone calling her name.

She pulled on the heavy door, but it wouldn't budge. Her head and chest ached with excruciating pain. She was freezing cold, and her heart pounded heavily with each breath she took. Exhausted, her knees sagged, and she slipped soundlessly to the floor. She felt strong arms pick her up and carry her, and she recognized the smell of Duke's shirt. She opened her eyes to look at him. He was crying. *Poor Duke! He is always savin' my skin.* But Duke hadn't been quick enough this time. Mollie's eyes closed again for the last time.

*****

The phone by the bed rang shrilly, and Gil forced himself awake. It rang twice more before he could pick it up.

"Mr. Hayworth, this is Duke."

"Duke? What's the trouble?" He squinted to read the numbers on the clock on the bedside table. It was not even midnight. He hadn't been asleep very long.

"You better come," Duke said. "It's Mollie."

Gil's mind was having trouble computing. "Where are you, Duke?"

"At the hospital." Gil realized that the old man was crying.

"I'll be right there," he told him as he slipped out of his warm bed.

Pam was struggling into her robe. "Is it Mollie?"

"It must be. Duke sounded upset."

"I'm going with you."

Gil didn't argue. "I'll wake the others," he told her.

In less than fifteen minutes, two cars were on their way to the hospital. All three children had insisted on going. Gil didn't have the heart to tell them that they couldn't. As they drove through a drizzly Grayport night, the Christmas lights, strung across the deserted city streets, glistened eerily.

At the hospital, Duke was waiting at the front entrance. Gil knew by the look on Duke's face that something terrible had happened. He put his arm around the old man and led him inside to the lobby.

"Somehow she got outta bed," Duke explained to them. "They don't know how. When I came to see her, she wasn't in her bed. I ran into the hall and saw her by the stairway door. I hollered like the dickens, but she was tryin' to get the door open when she fell. I thought she'd passed out, so I carried her back to her room. The nurse told me she was gone." Tears engulfed him. "She's dead, Mr. Hayworth," he sobbed, his shoulders shaking.

Gil swallowed hard and turned around to find his family and the two visitors standing behind him. They had all heard Duke's words. Carl Norris's face was pale, and Ed Patterson had his arm around him, comforting him. Tears filled Pam's eyes as she led the children to another corner of the hospital lobby. Only Gil, Carl Norris, and Duke got on the elevator to go to Mollie's room.

Gil pulled the sheet away from Mollie's face, and for the first time since he'd first seen her back in September, the lines had disappeared from her face, and she was at peace. On the bedside table, he spotted the wrinkled piece of paper propped up against the vase of carnations that he and Pam had brought earlier. The writing was hard to read. Gil struggled to make out the words.

Frend, he read. *Tnx. I no now.* It was signed M. Norris.

"She remembered," Gil said softly and passed the wrinkled paper to Carl Norris. The man clutched it to his breast.

Gil left Duke, Carl Norris, and Ed Patterson with Mollie and rejoined his family in the waiting room. Boyd sat in a corner chair, thumbing through a magazine, tears in his eyes. Traci was slouched on a long couch, her eyes closed. Gil knew she wasn't asleep. Tim stood before the watercolor print on the wall, looking but not really seeing. Gil walked over to stand beside him.

"Tim, I know what you're thinking, and none of this was your fault."

"But, Dad, I'm the one who told Bailey about Mollie. He would never have bothered her otherwise."

"You don't know that for sure. We still don't know if Bailey and his friends did this to her."

"Yes, I do, and now Mollie's dead because of me."

"Tim, she had pneumonia long before she was roughed up. The doctor told your mom that the pneumonia was really bad. The beating, though brutal, was not what did the real damage to Mollie's body."

Tim turned to look at Gil. "Are you sure? Or are you just trying to make me feel better?"

"Tim, you can ask the doctor yourself. Mollie was really ill before those thugs broke into the hotel. Believe me, Tim."

Though it would be a while before Tim accepted the truth, Gil knew that eventually he'd forgive himself. On the other hand, would any of them be able to forgive Bailey Nickerson if, indeed, he was the guilty one? They'd try, but it would be hard.

Gil was thankful for the change in his family over the past few months. They were so much closer now, and without Mollie even knowing it, she had done that for them.

Mollie would bring changes to Carl Norris's family, too, even though he didn't have a chance to get reacquainted with his mother. He would have to accept the way she had lived for the past forty years, and forgiveness for not searching for her would not come easy. But Ed Patterson was a good friend. He would help him through the rough days ahead. Mollie had brought them together, too, to form a bond of friendship. Gil was awed by how many people one life could touch without even being aware of it. Thank goodness, God knows.

A nurse, holding an armload of tattered clothing, appeared in front of them. "These are Mollie's things," she said, holding them out to Gil. "I thought you might want them, Mr. Hayworth."

Gil reached out for the few items of clothing and the green rubber boots. The Navy pea jacket was covered with blood. As he clutched it to his heart, his emotions tearing him apart, he felt something lumpy in one of the pockets. He pulled out a crumpled pink carnation and instantly lost control. Through the tears, he realized that even if it was food and clothing she needed, the flowers had made Mollie happy. She had packed that one single flower in her pocket to remind her that she had a friend.

19

The next week passed in a jumble of emotions. Christmas Day came and went without much notice. Preparations were made by an unhappy but gracious woman at the mortuary who realized that getting Mary Margaret Norris on a flight back to Missouri was urgent. She and her husband put their Christmas plans on hold and did all that was necessary to see to it that Mollie was on the same plane bound for St. Louis as her son and his friend, Ed Patterson.

Gil wondered if Avery Norris would ever believe the fantastic story his son would tell him, and would he be able to close the chapter in his life that had brought him so much pain? Carl Norris had forgiven his mother. Perhaps Avery Norris would be able to do the same. Mollie would never have left the family that she loved. They would surely realize that now.

Finally, after days of turmoil, the Hayworth family was at SeaTac Airport to give Mollie her send-off. Carl Norris offered his hand to Gil.

"Thank you for everything," he said. "This didn't work out like either of us planned, and I regret that, but at least we know that my mother remembered who she was before she died. Duke told me how important that was to her. Maybe now she knows who I am too." He wrapped his arms around Gil in a hug. Ed Patterson gave each of them a hug and both men walked through the boarding area to the plane.

The Hayworths watched and waited silently until the plane that carried Mollie home had taxied down the long runway, rose majestically into the air, and disappeared into the clouds over Seattle.

As they all stared into the empty sky, Gil asked, "Is anyone hungry?"

Gil was visualizing steak and prawns with a baked potato at one of the airport's main restaurants, but Traci piped up "McDonald's is open," and her brothers both nodded in agreement. Gil looked at Pam who just shrugged her "don't care" look.

Gil didn't mind. He was so thankful for his family and how much they'd cared for Mollie, that, at the moment, he'd allow them to eat anything.

*****

Duke took a few plates from the huge stack of dirty dishes and dropped them into the large sink of soapy water. It was his job to get the kitchen cleaned up after breakfast. As he swabbed each plate with the soapy brush, he thought about Mollie and all that had happened in the last few days, and tears ran down his cheeks. Christmas had come and gone, and now Mollie was gone too. She wasn't even in a cemetery where he could go visit. She was just gone. He would miss her so much. He'd felt responsible for her for so long even though she pretty much took care of herself. Now he was all alone. He hadn't made many friends in Grayport, but he would never leave this place.

Nope, he'd just live day by day until his old bones gave out, like Mollie's. Probably folks at the Mission would see to his burial.

Mollie's son had come to the Mission the day after Mollie passed to talk with him. He'd wanted to know everything that had happened from the first night in Joplin to the day he'd carried her back to her room and laid her frail body in the hospital bed. He tried to tell the man as much as he could remember. He knew they'd taken Mollie to Seattle yesterday. They'd invited him to go along, but he'd told 'em no.

He heard his name mentioned out front like someone was lookin' for him. He dried his hands and stuck his head out of the kitchen.

Gil Hayworth came toward him. "Duke, if you can get away, we'd like you to come to our house for a very late Christmas celebration. Pam's fixing a tasty ham dinner for all of us. And can you imagine? Those kids haven't opened their gifts yet? I'm supposed to get you and get back home as fast as I can. They're anxious. We even have some gifts under the tree for you."

One of the other men came up behind Gil and motioned to Duke. "Get outta here, fella! We'll finish the dishes for you."

Duke slowly removed his apron, took his coat from the rack on the wall, and followed Gil through the dining hall, out to the car. He felt like smiling.

Mebbe I'm not goin' to be alone now, he thought. *Mebbe after all these years, I'm goin' to have a family.* As he climbed into the front seat of the white sedan, he blinked away the tears, not wanting Mr. Hayworth to notice. But Gil did notice, and his heart swelled with happiness, knowing that through Duke, some part of Mollie's life would live on for all of them.

About the Author

Edie Johnson has wanted to be a writer since she was in high school in Kansas, over fifty years ago. Though she has written prolifically, nothing ever met with much success. Eventually, she married a sailor and moved to the Pacific Northwest where she raised three beautiful girls, all grown now with husbands and children of their own. Six years ago, she lost her husband of fifty-three years and now spends her time writing, often rewriting what she has already written. She finds writing to be a fulfilling pastime.

CPSIA information can be obtained
at www.ICGtesting.com
Printed in the USA
LVHW031417191220
674606LV00004B/774

9 781643 349121